Runaway Heart

Phyllis Kerr

Runaway Heart

Copyright ©2019 by Phyllis Kerr

All Rights Reserved

ISBN 978-0-578-67158-1

DEDICATION

To Mickey, Justin and Jesse

Love You Forever

Table of Contents

Chapter I

London, England

1859

Catherine Wilmershire paused in her re-waxing of the dining room table. It was strange, she thought peering down into the depth of its rich red finish, how her father's death had come as such a surprise. After all he had been deteriorating slowly since his brain hemorrhage over seven years ago. And for the past two years, he had been totally helpless having to be fed and changed like a baby. She had known for years he was dying. But it was still a surprise.

"Let Go!"

"I won't!"

The two female voices came from the parlor.

"There they go again," Cathy thought, "fighting over something of Father's, no doubt."

A strand of bright chestnut hair dangled behind her left ear. She reached up and tucked it back into the bun at the back of her neck.

"Why does it have to be this way?" she thought dismally. If Great Grandfather had not been so fond of gambling there might have been a little of the Wilmershire fortune left for them. As it was when Grandfather had inherited, all that remained was the country house in Corby and the small townhouse in London. He sold the estate in Colby and banked the money and it had been a good thing. For when he was suddenly struck down in the very prime of life, he left Father with five young children and a wife with no means of support. We would have been forced out on the streets to sell flowers or into service had it not been for the small monthly allowance Father drew from the proceeds of the sale. It had gotten them through the years.

Cathy sighed and smoothed a wrinkle from her navy-blue gown.

They had been lean and lonely years. There had been no money to hire maids or nurses so Cathy being the oldest girl, had gotten the jobs. At the age of thirteen she became cook, maid and nanny to the three younger children. Leonard, her older brother, could have helped, she thought, but whenever she had dared to suggest it, he would fly into a fury.

"Why should I wipe dirty behinds and scrub floors?" he would say in that superior manner he had

2

always used, even when he was a small child. I am the man of the house, the heir. I will not do woman's work. And their mother had always concurred.

Cathy smiled remembering the day she had suggested that if he were the master of this grand estate, perhaps he should lift a finger to maintain it. She had gotten her face slapped for her insolence but it had been worth it. At least she had spoken her mind.

"I said let go."

"I found it and it's mine." Her sister's shouts came from the parlor again.

"Stop that fussing," Cathy called out to them hoping they would stop quarrelling of their own accord before they disturbed their mother resting upstairs in her room. However, deep down she knew they wouldn't. They never did.

Cathy sighed again.

"Yes," she thought, "It had seemed a long hard time."

She had endured it the best that she could. But now Father was gone. Her brothers and sisters were all grown. Leonard had married and moved out of the house two years ago taking part of their household money with him. But he had returned this morning with his wife and new baby to claim his inheritance and officially take over as head of the family. At age eighteen it was time for her to think about her future. She was sure Leonard expected her to continue as cook and maid but she wanted to move on, face the world and see if she could stand on her own. Surely, life had more to offer than this.

A loud crash came from the parlor. Cathy rolled her eyes up toward the ceiling and threw down her dust cloth, then hesitated a moment. What would happen if she just let them fight to the death? she wondered, then decided against it. Mother would just hold her responsible for her dead sisters and the mess in the parlor, she thought.

"No, it would be easier to stop them now." She decided.

'Stop this instant," she yelled as she strode down the hall into the parlor.

Her sisters stood in the center of the room both holding fast to some small object.

As she drew nearer, she recognized the object between them. It was Father's favorite hairbrush. The one with the gold handle. She wrenched it from them.

"What do you think you are doing? Teresa, why aren't you upstairs moving Charlotte's things into your room?"

Charlotte stomped her foot defiantly. "I don't want to share a room with Teresa. Her room is like a pig sty."

"Well, where is Leonard going to sleep if you don't give him your room?" Cathy tried to reason with her.

Teresa, never one to let an insult go by, clenched her fist and waved it in Charlotte's face. "Pig sty! I'll show you pig sty."

"What the devil?" Leonard said sauntering into the room. "It's impossible to rest in this house with you screech owls going on."

Cathy turned toward him, her very last bit of patience gone.

"It's disgraceful. Father is only in his grave three weeks and these too are fighting over his hairbrush." Leonard laughed sarcastically.

"There is no fight. It's my brush. I now own this house and everything in it. It is mine as rightful heir.

Charlotte ignored his claim and expertly changed the subject.

"Oh Leonard, I don't want to share a room with Teresa." Her lower lip protruded into a pout. "Why do you have to move in here with us? There's not enough room for you and Margarite and baby Trevor."

"Because now that I have inherited, my debtors expect me to pay up. I simply can't afford to maintain two households. Besides, Mother wants me here." Leonard plopped down in the nearest chair.

"Would somebody shut that baby up, please." Marcus grumbled as he walked into the room carrying his empty sherry bottle. His words slurred as if he had spent the entire night drinking. "He is squalling like a mating cat."

Cathy knew she should hold her tongue, but she had had enough.

"Can't Margarite see to her son? She hasn't risen from that bed since she arrived early this morning."

Margarite is not expected to perform household chores." Leonard said as if astounded anyone would even consider the idea. "Cathy, that shall be one of your new duties."

Cathy's body stiffened and it was all she could do to keep from giving them all a good going over with the gold brush she had taken from her sisters.

"Leonard," she said taking a stand for herself for the first time in her life, "I will not be nursemaid to your son while you and your wife loll around the house like Lord and Lady Wilmershire."

Leonard lifted one eyebrow and slanted his lips in a bored smile.

"You will if you wish to live in this house," he said.

Cathy wanted to scream at him, all of them, who will take care of you if I am not here? But she knew they did not care if she was here or not.

"Then I'll be leaving. You can all take care of yourselves," she said not even trying to hide her hurt and resentment.

Charlotte and Teresa's eyes grew large and they looked at each other.

"No Leonard, don't let her go," they begged. "I can move in with Teresa," Charlotte said. "I really don't mind."

Leonard thought for a moment.

"You know", he said slowly. You have struck on a good solution to a quandary I have been dealing with. Do you remember Peter Weston, a friend of mine from school?"

Cathy nodded yes.

"I can send the Westons a letter that you are coming for a visit. I have joined with Peter and a group of his friends in a business venture. I cannot leave London until I have officially documented my heirship in the Royal Archives. You could have a nice visit and get to know Peter."

She looked at Leonard with contempt.

"You make me sick, all of you. You must be the laziest and most selfish, self-centered people on this world!"

She turned to leave but a loud whack echoed through the room. Cathy covered her stinging cheek with her hand. She hadn't heard her mother come up behind her. She always looked austere, but completely dressed in the voluminous black gown of mourning, she looked every bit the shroud of death.

"Don't you ever talk that way about your family," Racine Wilmershire said in her quietly dignified voice that wore like fine sand across Cathy's nerves. She

8

had a cool edge about her which had always made Cathy feel emotionally distant from her.

"Your family loves you," Mrs. Wilmershire said. "It is your sour temperament that brings disquiet to this household."

Seeing her advantage, Charlotte reached out and snatched the gold hairbrush out of Cathy's hand. Cathy pushed past her mother and walked out of the room.

"Always was too damned high strung," Marcus said tucking a full bottle of sherry under his arm.

Cathy ran up the back stairs to her attic room. She slumped down into the worn blue chair in front of the dormer window and stared out at the drizzling London sky. Dusk was slowly fading into night and the cold February wind rattled a loose pane. It had been a cold wet winter. It was hard to remember that March was only three months away.

"I don't understand those people," she thought. "There would be no shame in Leonard and Marcus taking employment as a law clerk or bookkeeper to some fine families. The money would support the household comfortably. The girls could have a tutor to refine their social skills. Maybe they could have a London season. Many good matches grow from a round of dances and entertainments. But Father had raised his sons to believe that to work was below the family position in society."

"The Wilmershires were descended from a noble Saxon knight who rode side by side with King Edward the Confessor, the last of the great Saxon kings," he would say. "This knight, Sir Grunwald of Dortsmith was a fierce warrior. None could best him in battle. He filled the king's coffers with treasure and led the Saxons to many victories. The King rewarded him for his strength and loyalty with a kingdom of his own with fertile grounds and plenty of animals to hunt to support his family and vassals."

"Now this knight, Sir Grunwald, married a lowly Irish wench with eyes as green as the Emerald Isles and hair as red as the fires of Hell. She was a wild beauty, smart, strong of will and filled with passion but none dared love her. For when provoked, her raging temper flared with a burning vengeance that could scorch old Satan himself. Only Sir Grunwald dared claim her, for his strength was as great as her will. And when she raged, he turned her rage with his passion and they spent many warm nights together. It is told many children came of that union.

"Then he would look down at his children's wideeyed faces and point at her brothers and sisters. "You are all sprung from the loins of the great Saxon knight." They would raise their heads and smile proudly at one another.

Then Father would smile at Cathy with that enigmatic smile of his and say, "And you are from the low Irish wench," then chuckle as if at a jest.

"Foolishness," she always thought, "silly children's stories," but it was like her father always told her. She was different from the others. And although she never said it, she felt different. She even looked different. Where they were short and stout with golden blonde hair. She was taller and fine-boned with brown hair, a light English brown, with tinges of red spun through. And where they had clear blue eyes, she had a blue-green that changed with her moods and could easily be read by anyone who knew her.

Cathy watched as a single drop of rain splashed against the window then made its jagged way down to the sill. She was weary of them. Weary of this house, weary of the work, and weary of the endless bickering. She needed a break. She longed to make a journey somewhere, anywhere. But when could she go with everything at odds here in the house?

"But why does she have to wait?" she thought. Let them settle things. Let them see to the house. Let them see firsthand just how hard it is to take care of them.

She sat up. "She could go to the Weston's for a visit," she thought. Although she did not know them very well, Mr. and Mrs. Weston had seemed like agreeable people when they had come to visit some years ago. She did not remember the children, Sylvia and Peter, but they were adults by now. Peter must be close to twenty-four and Sylvia eighteen, she calculated. They had spent most of their young lives in boarding schools in Paris. And she remembered Sylvia had been a sickly child. Cathy wondered if she could help Sylvia in some way, maybe be her companion. The idea sounded perfect. She had the small trust her grandmother had left her. She wouldn't have to depend on Leonard for anything. She could leave tonight. No one would know she had left until morning.

Cathy's mood lightened. An inner excitement coursed through her tired body. She jumped out of her chair and set right to work. She opened the old-fashioned trunk that always sat at the foot of her bed. She took her few self-made gowns out of the makeshift wardrobe and folded them into the trunk. Not wanting to ruin her best shoes in the rain, she packed them with her gowns, put in her few toilet articles then sat back on her heels looking at the battered trunk. It was the same one her grandmother used sixty years ago to pack her trousseau at the age of fourteen. "I wonder what grandmother thought as she sat looking at her future in this very same case."

"So many old memories," Cathy thought. She slammed the top closed. It was time to make her own new memories. She returned to the chair in front of the window and waited for the house to grow quiet.

Several hours passed before the thumping of activity stopped and the house fell silent. Only the occasional pop of a settling wall and the gentle tapping of the rain could be heard. Cathy tied the cords of her cape tightly then opened her door and looked out. Finding the stairway empty, she hooked her right arm through the leather strap that encircled the trunk and lifted as hard as she could. The trunk was heavy but she was able to carry it to the edge of the stairs. She grasped the strap with her left hand and using her body for leverage, she lowered the trunk step by step until she slowly made it to the bottom.

From there, in the dark, the front door seemed miles away. "How was she going to carry the heavy trunk that far?" she wondered. She bent down and felt around on the floor for something to use. Her hand ran up against the throw rug that crossed from the parlor to the dining room. She lifted the edge of the wool rug and tugged at it until it sat right beside the trunk. She stood and it took all her strength to lift the trunk. She had planned to place it quietly on the rug, but she could not hold it. It slipped out of her hands and hit the floor with a thud. Cathy froze in place, held her breath, hoping no one heard. The house remained silent so, quickly, she placed both hands on the trunk and pushed. It slid noiselessly to the front door.

Suddenly remembering she had no money, she hurried to her mother's desk in the parlor. She opened the bottom drawer and took out the black lacquered jewel box where her mother kept the household cash. She ruffled through the bills, pulled out a twenty-pound note and replaced the box closing the drawer gently. "This will get me to the Westons." She thought. When I get settled, I can make arrangements to have my money transferred to a bank there.

Content with her plan, she went back to the trunk. With much tugging, pushing, and coaxing, Cathy maneuvered it to the end of the front walk. The rain fell harder than she had expected. She covered her head with the hood on the cloak and pulled the cape tightly around her. A shiny black coach lumbered up the street toward her. She waved her arms in the air trying to get the driver's attention. Her cape fell open. The rain drenched her face and the front of her dress. Holding the cape shut with her left hand she waved with her right but it did no good. The shadowy coach rumbled on by. A few minutes later another coach came up the street. She jumped up and down and waved but it too passed by leaving momentary tracks in the rain water as it continued down the street.

Cathy sat down on her trunk and waited. The wetness began to seep through her cape bringing the chilled night with it. Her bare hands were already red and stiff and she flexed her fingers trying to coax the blood back into them.

"This will give them something to laugh about," she thought only half joking. "I pack my bag and run away, then freeze to death on the front stoop."

15

Just then she spotted another coach moving slowly up St. Charles and determined not to be passed by a third time, Cathy jumped up and ran out into the street. She planted her feet firmly beneath her and thought, "this coach will have to stop or run me down." It came closer and closer. She held up her hands and the dripping horse came to a halt in front of her.

"Are you for hire? She called out to the driver.

"Aye," a gruff voice said from under the black stovepipe hat.

"I have a trunk," she said pointing to where it sat on the front walk.

The driver climbed down and loaded the trunk onto the back of the coach. Cathy opened the door and put her foot on the step then turned around to take one last look at her home. A movement in the window of Charlotte's room caught her eye and for a minute she thought she saw Leonard peeping out at her, smiling smugly.

"Oh, you're just imagining things," she thought laughing at herself. She climbed into the coach.

"Black Ball Shipping Office," she said to the driver and the coach pulled out and headed for the docks.

Chapter II

The inside of the coach was just as cold as the outside, and only slightly less damp. Cathy was relieved to hear the tiny brass bell tinkle as she closed the shipping office door behind her. The potbellied baseburner crackled warmly in the middle of the room. Her fingers and nose ached from the cold. The radiating heat pulled her toward its source. Someone cleared his throat and she turned to see a man standing only a head above the counter, a visor cap shadowing his face, looking at her over gold wire rimmed bifocals. She had walked right passed him and hadn't seen him.

"May I help you?" he said.

"Yes," Cathy said taking the twenty-pound note out of her cloak pocket. "I would like to book passage to the colonies, America, I mean." "Where in America?" he asked.

"Texas," she said.

He walked over to a desk covered with schedules and charts. He picked up one schedule, then another, then another reading each one closely, first with his glasses on, then with his glasses off. Finally, he set them down and came back.

"I can book you on the Lady Lane leaving port next Tuesday," he said looking up at her through his thick glasses.

Cathy's heart leaped.

"Next Tuesday!"

The clerk took a step backward.

Cathy hadn't meant to yell at him.

"Sorry," she said. "I need to leave tonight."

The clerk drew his brows together and squinted one impatient eye at her then went back to the desk and picked up two schedules bringing them almost to the tip of his nose. He examined each one closely, as if there was something between the fibers which he hadn't previously seen then put them down, scratched his balding head and returned to Cathy.

"I can book you on the Europa. It's my first packet leaving for America but she won't take you straight to Texas. First, she goes to New York, then to New Orleans, then docks in Galveston, Texas."

"How long will it take?" she asked.

18

"About six weeks." he replied. "But she doesn't leave until tomorrow at twelve noon," he added quickly.

Cathy's heart sank. What was she going to do? She didn't have enough money for decent lodgings for the night.

"Don't you have anything for tonight, anything at all?" She pleaded.

"Sorry. Only thing leaving tonight is a clipper but she's carrying cargo and mail, no passengers."

He looked at her square in the face, his narrow jaw set firm. She knew it was no use to argue with him.

"How long will it take the clipper to cross?" she asked.

"Three weeks."

"Is it too late to post a letter for the clipper?"

The clerk sighed in exasperation. He seemed to want this business done. "Not if you hurry, Miss." He reached under the counter and pulled out a piece of paper and pen.

"At least I can send a letter to the Weston's telling them I am coming," she thought. "And I'll take that ticket for the Europa," she said.

When she finished the letter, she gave it to the clerk. He posted it and put it with the rest of the mail to be loaded on the clipper. She paid for the ticket, put in her cloak pocket and turned to leave but stopped. Grandmother's trunk sat in the middle of the floor where the coachman had left it.

"She couldn't carry it around with her until the ship sailed," she thought.

She turned back to the clerk. He had just sat back down and propped his feet up on top of the desk.

"Would you please see that this is put on the Europa?" she said pointing at the trunk.

The little clerk peered at her over his bifocals, his mouth pressed into a straight line.

"Yes, Miss," he said letting his feet fall to the floor. "I'll take care of it for you."

"Thank you," she said and the little bell tinkled again as she closed the office door behind her.

Outside, the steady rain had turned into a heavy fog. The wet streets looked like mirrors reflecting the gray void that hovered above them. The darkness made Cathy nervous. She could hear people mumbling but she couldn't see anyone. She was alone in her small circle of invisibility. Fear shivered down her spine and she pulled her cloak tighter around her in search of security as well as warmth.

"I'll never find my way in this mess," she thought looking out into the darkness that surrounded her. Not knowing what else to do, she sat down on the office step and let her head fall against the building.

Fatigue tugged at her eyelids.

"It's late," she thought, trying to get her bearings. A faint light glowed in the distance, a street lamp, she thought. She could go from street lamp to street lamp. Eventually she would run into an inn. A room would probably cost too much but maybe she could wait in the lobby or dining hall for the remainder of the night or at least until the sun came up. It wasn't a very good plan and she didn't relish the idea of walking through the dark stretches alone but there was nothing else she could do. She couldn't spend the night here. She stood, shook the dampness from her skirts, and stepped down to the walkway.

Suddenly, the world went black. Her arms were stuck to her sides, her breath clogged in her throat. She was inside something. A bag! she realized. Then hands were on her. Large, rough hands. Two around her shoulders, two around her ankles. She was being lifted. She felt the ground leave her feet and she was being carried, fast, head first. Scream! She thought. Scream! But before she could utter a sound, she was swung up and then dropped hard on her back, the impact knocking the wind out of her.

She lay there, dazed. She felt a lurch then a swaying motion. The hollow clop of animal hooves hitting wet stones beat against her ears. She was in some kind of coach or wagon and it was moving.

"My God, what is happening?" she thought trying to sit up but the hands pushed her back down.

21

Stay down, my beauty," a reedy voice said. "We ain't going to hurt you – if you behave."

Cathy knew real fear for the first time in her life. Her heart pounded against her chest so hard she was sure it would burst. She strained her eyes trying to see through the coarse bag that covered her head and half of her body but she saw only blackness.

The coach stopped and Cathy heard the door open.

"Give us her handbag," a low voice, meaner sounding than the first, said. Hands pulled at her skirt and cloak, running over her body like rats in a sewer.

"It ain't here, the man inside said.

"What do you mean it ain't here?" the other man mimicked him. He stepped into the coach and looked around rolling Cathy from side to side as he searched.

"What are you up to?" he said ominously, taking his hands from her. She heard a loud crash, like wood cracking, and the coach rocked beneath her.

"You holding out on me?" the lower voice said.

Cathy could tell by the tone of his voice that he was not a man to be crossed.

"I swear, I ain't. Search me. I ain't got it. She must've dropped it back there."

Cathy wanted to tell them there was no handbag but her fear plugged her throat and wouldn't let her speak.

Huh," the lower voice said. The voices paused a moment then she felt the motion of the coach as the two men climbed out. One of the men grasped her shoulders and dragged her out. Her feet glanced the ground as she was swept up into strong arms and crushed against a wall of chest that reeked of sweat and rancid tobacco. From somewhere not too far away, she heard a knock then felt herself being carried inside a building. She heard the door shut behind her. Heavy boots fell loudly on wooden floors, then became muted on carpet. She felt herself being placed in a chair.

"Don't you move," the lower voice said.

Feet shuffled, a door opened and shut. Cathy could hear voices in another room talking. She couldn't understand what they were saying. A wild, uninhibited laugh, a woman's laugh, vibrated through the walls.

"She had to do something, now!" she thought. She had to escape. Was anyone watching her? Thoughts swirled through her mind as panic climbed nearer to the surface.

Then the door swung open and the voices came closer. The strong scent of flowers filled the room. Cathy's heart froze.

"Well, Cherie, I am not going to pay for something I have not seen," a woman with a French accent said.
"Bring her in here."

Cathy was lifted one last time, and carried a short distance. Suddenly, she was flung into the air. She was falling! Terror gripped her and she reached out blindly, searching for anything to grab to stop the fall.

She landed with a whop in the middle of something large and soft.

Panic took full reign. Desperately she struggled with the bag trying to get it off but it was tangled up with her cloak and skirts. She pulled and pushed at the rough fabric burning her face and hands until finally she worked her hands and knees beneath her and, pushing up, managed to back out of the clinging prison.

In the soft pink light, she could finally see. She stood in the corner of a big bed, poised on the tips of her long slender fingers, her hair burning red in the dim light and knotted wildly around her face, her blue-green eyes open wide looking like some wild animal ready to attack anyone who came near.

Three people stood staring in front of her. Two men, one large and whiskered, the other smaller and toothless, dressed in sailor's clothes, and a woman with paper white skin wearing a matching white wig. Amusement wrinkled the corners of the woman's eyes. She threw her head back and her laughter shook the pink fringe on the red velvet lamp shades.

"Oh, yes, I will pay for this one," she said crossing to the armoire on the opposite side of the room and reaching in among dozens of pink dressing gowns, she pulled out a small leather pouch filled with coins.

At the sight of the money, the two men looked at each other and smiled. The larger one winked a piggish eye at his partner and sidled up to the woman, taking the pouch that dangled between her fingers.

He pulled the knit cap off his head and crumpled it against his grimy chest.

"Thank you, Miss Paulette."

The woman fluttered her heavily mascaraed eyes and curved her crimson lips up into a smile.

"You are welcome. Always come to me first. You will find I pay better than anyone on the street."

The man nodded his head backing out of the door and the smaller man followed, neither giving Cathy even a sideways glance.

Now they were alone, Paulette turned her full attention to Cathy.

"There, there pretty one. You don't have to be afraid of me."

She moved over to the bed and Cathy pulled back as far away as she could until her back was flat against the wall. The soft voice sounded sympathetic but Cathy did not trust her.

Realizing this, Paulette sat on the side of the bed and patted the spot beside her.

"Come, child, I only want to talk. These men, they have scared you. But see, I have sent them away. Come on."

Cathy eyed Paulette warily. She wanted to trust her. She wanted to believe that this woman would help her but instinct and just plain fear kept her motionless. She had been abducted and brought here for a reason. She was not moving from this spot until she knew why.

"What do you want from me?" Cathy asked trying to sound bold but her voice cracked and she sounded more like she was going to cry than demand explanations.

Paulette's voice became almost motherly.

"Why, you are frightened. But you are safe here." She reached out and pulled the bell cord hanging beside the bed. A girl in a maid uniform entered.

"Bring some tea for the young lady," Paulette told the maid in her heavy French accent. The maid curtsied and left. Paulette smiled at Cathy.

"Some nice hot tea will do you good. You are cold and confused."

The maid returned with the tea and handed it to Miss Paulette then left.

"Come and sit by me. Drink your tea and I will explain everything to you."

Cathy looked at the steaming cup Paulette held out to her. "She shouldn't take it," she thought, but the warm fragrance drifted up to her. She hadn't eaten any dinner and the wet chill of the night still clung to her. Physical need overcame common sense. She moved within arm's length of Paulette and took the tea. She took a few sips. It tasted bitter but warm.

"You will feel better now. Much more relaxed," Paulette said taking the cup from her hands.

Paulette was right, she thought. The tea was beginning to relax her all over.

"I'll be able to think more clearly now," she thought. Her eyelids started to feel heavy. She rubbed them trying to rub away the sudden grogginess coming over her. Cathy looked at Paulette. Her face seemed to be nearer than it was before. Up close, she looked wrinkled, old. The black heart shaped beauty spot at the edge of her mouth jumped up and down when she talked.

"You are tired. Why don't you just lay back and take a little nap," Paulette said softly.

"Sleep. That's what she needed. If she could just sleep for a little while, Cathy thought. She stretched out on the bed and sank down into the soft pink covers. They smelled of men's bodies and a strange heavy perfume. Paulette's voice came to her from out of the distance and skimmed along the edges of her consciousness.

"Don't worry, Pretty One. I will take care of you. It will be easy the first time. I will see to it."

And with that, the voice disappeared in a swirl of pink smoke.

Chapter III

Cathy lay on the floor of the forest and looked up at the clear evening sky. A cool breeze slid between the tall evergreens starting their nightly whispers and passing over Cathy's naked body like a cloth of finest silk. In the distance, a nightingale began his lonesome song.

"Grand old Sally,

Working Tucker's alley,

Line up with your shilling,

Old Sally's always willing!"

The off-key voices interrupted Cathy's dream and pulled at her consciousness as the words circled around and around in her head. Loud, familiar laughter vibrated through her haze. A nagging thought teased her mind then danced merrily out of reach. She needed to remember something-something important. What was it? She tried desperately to think but her mind would not focus. It took too much effort and she was so tired. She just wanted to sleep, to go back to her beautiful dream.

She felt her legs nudged apart and the cool evening air caressed her intimately. A wonderful longing came over her. Hands stroked her thighs. Not grabbing, hurting hands, but gentle soothing hands, massaging every inch of her, awakening a physical need for something as yet unknown. Soft lips nibbled her feet, her stomach, her breasts, her neck taunting her senses until she felt she could stand no more. A weight lowered onto her and she moved in harmony with her longing. A face drifted into focus, beautiful brown eyes filled with passion and half closed with pleasure. Just as it came, the face faded away and all that mattered was the need to quench the mounting desire within her. Suddenly her body exploded with pleasure, a wonderful, liberating pleasure that freed her from desire and left her drifting on the night breezes. Darkness came and went and visions tumbled over one another until finally she sank back into the euphoric splendor of black, dreamless sleep.

Ray Michaels awoke. He pulled himself up in the creaky old four poster and leaned back against the rough mahogany headboard, swallowing twice, trying to moisten the cotton that stuck to the roof of his mouth and hung along the edges of his swollen tongue. He looked around the cold empty room and spotted a pitcher of water sitting on a lopsided table, probably not fit to drink, he thought running his hands through his black hair and swinging his long muscular legs over the side of the bed. He stood and peered suspiciously into the pitcher. Nothing moved so he raised it to his mouth and gulped thirstily. A small stream of water rolled down his stubbly chin and dripped onto his furry chest. He set down the pitcher and rubbed the black curly hair dry with his palms. A chill started up his bare legs so he stepped back to the bed and hurriedly pulled the covers up around his waist.

"How did I end up in this dump?" Ray wondered staring at the peeling wallpaper, trying to sort through the fuzzy events of the night before. He had been awfully drunk. It was his friend Dan's idea. He remembered stumbling into the brightly lit room filled with men and scantily dressed girls and announcing to the crowd, "I'll have the most expensive girl in the house!" The white haired madame stepped out of a group of men laughing loudly and motioning at a tall butler standing in the corner.

"Mr. Dobbs, show this man up." She said.

Ray looked down at the sleeping form beside him. "She had been well worth the price," he thought. Sleepy sea green eyes, supple firm body, long silky legs, breasts like two juicy peaches, she tasted sweet all over, like honey. Her complexion was flawless and her thick lashes made a sable crescent along the edges of her closed eyes. Her straight nose curved up ever so slightly with a subtle flare at the nostrils. She was beautiful. Lying there asleep, she looked almost innocent. Ray smiled. Except for her mouth. Hers was not the mouth of an innocent.

He gathered a handful of long auburn hair and crushed it in his fist. He let his gaze wander down her back to the gentle curve of her hips. She had been so responsive, sensual last night. He let his gaze drop lower. Just the thought of those luscious thighs set him astir.

For the first time in a month, Ray realized, he was not in a hurry to go home. He wanted to get better acquainted with this beautiful lady, see if she has a mind as stunning as her body.

"Unfortunately, there's not enough time," he thought.

In a few hours he would be sailing for home. He still had a lot to do, not the least of which was to find Dan who, when Ray last saw him, was even drunker than he was. Reluctantly, he released the shining hair, straining its softness through his fingers. He jumped out of bed and picked his clothes up off the floor where he had thrown them last night. He pulled on his shirt leaving it unbuttoned and rolling up his sleeves, he poured some water into the white porcelain bowl to wash his face and hands.

Cathy rolled onto her back and slowly opened her sleep heavy eyes. "What a strange dream," she thought uncurling her arms and legs and stretching them out straight like a cat awakening from a long nap. A dull ache pounded at the base of her skull and she tried to sit up but the room spun around her. Then a searing pain shot up the back of her neck to the top of her head. She pressed both hands to her forehead and fell back on the bed.

Ray chuckled and wiping his hand on a dirty towel, walked over to the bed smiling down at the suffering beauty below him.

"Good morning. Looks like you drank too much last night, too."

Cathy stared up at the lazy brown eyes above her.

Those eyes," She thought. "They are the same eyes that were in my dream! How could that be?" Her eyes widened, "unless that was not a dream!"

Still smiling, Ray strode back to the table, threw down the towel and took his wallet out of his coat pocket.

"I wanted to buy you something special, a gift in appreciation for last night. I'm leaving for America in a few hours and I don't have time for shopping."

He pulled several bills out of the brown leather case and walked back to the bed.

Cathy watched him warily as he moved around the room. She would have to challenge him physically to reach the door and it was probably locked anyway. Her instincts told her to keep quiet and be ready to run at the first opportunity.

Ray noted the stressed look on her face.

"This will buy you something pretty." He set the money on the end table.

Then to her surprise, he reached down and peeled the covers away from her. As soon as he looked at her tempting body, he knew he shouldn't have. Just one look and he was ready for her again. He brushed the backs of his fingers against one soft nipple and his loins throbbed for the feel of her.

Cathy tried not to cringe. She wanted to scream at him, "Take your hands off me." But her instincts told her to be strong.

He slid his hand lower, passed her chest, across her belly, to the patch of hair down below.

Cathy couldn't stand it. She jerked away.

Ray looked up at her face wondering what was wrong. He took a step back looking concerned. Then he saw it. Red blood stains glared up at him from the white linen sheets. "Oh God," he thought. "this can't be." But the look on Cathy's face, like a trapped, wounded animal, confirmed it.

He didn't know what to say. Desire and compassion pulled him in opposite directions. He wanted to hold her, to comfort her, to take her again.

"You don't belong here, do you?" he asked hoping she could explain what was obviously true.

Cathy just stared with wide green eyes.

"Stay here. I'll be right back," he said through clenched teeth. He grabbed up his clothes and stalked out of the room leaving the door unlocked.

Cathy pressed her palms against her temples as hard as she could trying to clear her head. She heard loud arguing outside the room. The door opened. She feared it was the man coming back to rage at her. She pulled the covers tightly around her neck. But instead of the man, a young girl about sixteen years old, with black curly hair and a friendly smile stood just inside the door, a food tray in her hands.

Cathy stared at her for a minute, then sank back into bed, fighting the urge to break down and cry.

The girl set the tray on the table and sat down beside her.

"What is this? Come on, Dearie, that ain't going to do no good." Her voice soothed as she patted Cathy gently on the back. The friendly voice felt like a balm to her raw nerves. Cathy looked up at the pretty freckled face.

The girl smiled at her encouragingly and pulled a bundle from under her arm.

"Miss Paulette sent me up here with your clothes."

Cathy snatched the bundle out of the girl's arms and pressed it tightly against her chest.

"I'm Mazie. Who are you?" she said surprised at Cathy's modesty.

"Cathy," she replied looking over at the unlocked door.

"That's a pretty name." Mazie stood and walked to the table keeping her back to Cathy and busied herself with the teapot she had brought up on the tray.

Seeing her opportunity, Cathy climbed gingerly out of bed. She stepped into her petticoats and hurriedly pulled her rumpled navy-blue dress over her tangled hair.

Mazie looked up from the teapot.

"All dressed, eh?" She stepped around behind her and began fastening the catches. "Cheer up, Honey, this place ain't so bad. Look at me. I've been here two years and I'm doing fine. Why, if it hadn't been for Miss Paulette taking me in, I'd have starved to death out on the streets," she said brushing aside Cathy's knotted curls.

Finished with the dress, she guided Cathy to the only chair in the room.

"Sit here. Eat a slice of bread and butter. Drink some nice hot tea."

Cathy sat down and eyed the crust of bread on the tray.

Mazie lit the kerosene lamp sitting in the middle of the table and walked to the door. She wrapped one hand around the white ceramic knob, then stopped. She looked back at Cathy, a naughty smile playing at her lips.

"You know, you were lucky to have that tall, handsome Yankee all night. It must have really been something."

Cathy looked down and blushed to the very depth of her soul.

Mazie giggled impishly. "I thought so," she said opening the door and closing it gently behind her.

Cathy heard the lock click into place.

"Lucky?" She shifted in her chair trying to relieve the soreness between her legs. "Lucky?" she thought. She would laugh if she didn't feel so miserable. She picked up the cup of tea Mazie had poured for her. The warm fragrance drifted up her nostrils and suddenly her stomach retched. She dropped the cup and crossed both arms across her stomach, doubling over, trying to fight down the nausea. Gradually, it subsided and Cathy was able to sit up again.

"It was the tea," she thought remembering the same warm bitter fragrance from the night before. "She had drugged! Well, they weren't going to do it to her again!"

She pulled away from the spilled brew wiping both hands repeatedly on her skirt.

Carefully she reached over the mess and picked up the crust of bread. It was hard and stale but she had to have something to settle the roiling in her stomach. She raised the bread to her lips and a huge black cockroach crawled out of an air hole and leaped agilely onto her lap.

Cathy jumped to her feet and screamed hysterically. She threw the bread across the room and slapped wildly at the filthy creature that clung determinedly to her skirt. She managed to swat it to the floor where it scurried to the nearest corner and shinnied through a hairline crack in the wall. Cathy shook violently and clawed at her crawling skin. She felt as if thousands of hairy black feet scampered across her flesh.

"I've got to get out of here," she screamed running to the locked door. She pulled on the knob and beat against the solid wood until her hands were bruised and aching.

"Let me out," she screamed but no one came.

Desperately, she ran to the window and pulled at the boards that had been nailed across it. But it was no use. The window was nailed so solid that not even air or light could get in or out. Cathy spun around and paced back to the center of the room.

"I am not going to stay here another minute." She looked around trying to find something, anything to help her get out of that room. Her gaze locked onto her cloak lying on the bed where Mazie had left it. She ran over and fumbled through the pockets. There it was, she thought, her ticket for the Europa sailing today at noon. She clung to it as if her life depended on that small piece of paper.

"Twelve noon," she thought. "I have to be out of here at the latest by eleven thirty." She had no idea of the time right now.

"I have to think." She sat down on the bed and looked around the room again. She picked up her cloak and tied it around her shoulders then jumped out of the bed and ran to the wooden chair by the table. The chair was heavy but she managed to lift it once and slam it against the door as hard as she could. The blow jarred her arms up to her shoulders but the door stood immobile. She let the chair fall to the floor.

Only one thing held a chance of opening that door, she thought staring at the brightly burning flame of the kerosene lamp sitting on the table. Like a mad woman, she ran to the table, picked up the lamp, and carried it to the bed. Unscrewing the base, she poured kerosene over the sheets then, lifting the crystal, she threw the burning wick into the middle of the bed. It caught instantly. Smoke quickly filled the room. Cathy stepped back from the intensifying heat completely unmindful of the danger she was in.

"Fire, fire," she screamed.

No one came.

"Fire," she screamed again. The smoke was getting worse. Tears streamed from her eyes and her nose began to run. "My God, somebody open this door, there's a fire in here," she screamed.

She could feel the heat on her back growing. She turned around. The bed was completely consumed. Deadly fingers of smoke and flames reached out for more food to satisfy its raging hunger. Fear pricked at her panicked mind.

"What if nobody came?" she thought. "I'd rather die in this burning Hell than stay here and be treated like an animal," she swore. With renewed determination, she turned her back to the fire and began pounding on the door in earnest.

"Help me, please, help me," she screamed. To her surprise, someone pounded back. "In here, in here," she screamed.

The lock clicked and the door opened. Two young girls stood in the hall staring in horror and disbelief at the burning room. Both girls began to scream as they ran down the hall to the stairs then to the back of the house, screaming, "Miss Paulette! Miss Paulette! Fire!"

Cathy followed them as far as the bottom of the stairs, then made her way to the front entry hall. By then everyone in the house had been alerted. Men and girls alike rushed to the doors and out into the safety of the streets. Cathy moved along with them. Outside, men discreetly slipped away into waiting cabs or just disappeared into the chilly morning. The girls stood in a group watching the smoke that had begun to billow out of the top of the house. Soon other people began to come out of neighboring houses and businesses. Confusion and chaos became rampant as more people gathered to watch the old house burn.

Cathy looked at the other girls standing around her. Their eyes were on the fire. Slowly, careful not draw any attention to herself, Cathy took a step backward. No one paid her any mind. She took another step. Then another. She looked at the others again. They were still intent on the fire. She turned and began to walk in the direction of the docks. Her heart was pounding, her face was burned red from the exposure to the fire. She hadn't noticed before but she was walking in bare feet. She was hoping no one would notice either. She wanted to run, to get away as fast as she could, but she forced herself to walk.

A man passed by her.

"Excuse me, sir. What time do you have?" she asked trying to sound calm.

He pulled a watch from his pocket.

"A quarter to ten," he said without looking at her and hurried on his way toward the fire.

"A quarter to ten," she thought. She was going to make it! Relief flooded through her. Hysterical, mad laughter bubbled up inside her but she maintained her outward composure. Her fist closed tighter around the ticket she still held in her hand. "There's time for that later," she thought. She quickened her steps and headed straight for the docks never once looking back at the melee behind her.

41

Chapter IV

"Gosh, it feels good to be off that squeeze box," Dan Swenson said shaking his legs out, trying to shed the cramped feeling that sailing for long distances always gave him.

Raymond Michaels looked at the big Swede, amusement crinkled his lazy brown eyes.

Now how is it that a big Norseman like you with Viking blood flowing through his veins hates

sailing?" Dan drew his brows together and shook his head.

"That was them, not me. It isn't natural for a man to be cooped up in a little bitty space like that." He threw his arm up toward the ship.

"I need some room to roam. I'd take a horse between my legs to that any day."

Ray threw his head back and laughed heartily.

42

"I'm going on over to the hotel. Dad's supposed to meet me there. See that these men unload that cargo and be careful of those two bulls. After four weeks on this ship they're libel to be a little feisty. I don't want either one of 'em hurt."

Dan nodded his head.

"After that's done you can go on and do what you want to do but stay out of trouble."

Dan looked at Ray, a spark of mischief in his pale, blue eyes.

"In New Orleans?" he said. "There ain't no way."

Ray laughed again.

"We're leaving for home in three days so make the most of it." Leaving his trusted foreman to his work, he headed for the hotel.

Four weeks since he had left London, he thought as he walked along. Four weeks of rolling gray seas and blustery winds and not one night had passed that he hadn't thought about the green-eyed virgin at the brothel. The image of her lying there naked, looking so hurt and confused, left him feeling like she definitely needed help. But while he was trying to sort her story out with the madame, the fire broke out. He went to the room where he had left her but she was gone. No one remembered seeing her leave. One chamber maid said the girl's name was Cathy. He waited around to find out what information the madame had about her but to his frustration Madame

Paulette had left in a Hansom cab never to be seen again. He could only hope that Cathy had gotten away safely.

It was good to be back after the six months of travel. America had a strength and vitality about it that no other country could match. London had its bored sophistication and France its gaiety, but America was young and strong and Ray could feel it coursing through him, revitalizing him as he strode through the stream of busy people.

He turned onto Royal Street and walked up to the St. Louis hotel where he and his father always stayed in New Orleans. A crowd of men and women had gathered just outside the doors. A portly well-dressed man stood on an orange crate making a speech.

"And so, I say to you, my friends, that in these trying times, it is your duty, nay, your obligation to stand up and vote for the man who will deliver us from the darkness of despair to the sacred light of glory, the next President of the United States, Abraham Lincoln."

Ray watched in silent amusement as at the pronouncement of the last two words, a loud protest rose from the crowd and the speaker was unceremoniously knocked from his box onto the hard, red brick street. He scrambled to his feet to avoid being trampled only to find himself running for his life with two irate southern gentlemen chasing him, waving their clenched fists in the air. Ray was aware of the growing animas between southern plantation owners and northern politicians over the slavery problem. But a war? It didn't take a genius to come to the conclusion the practice is wrong. Human beings can't own other human beings. It's like trying to own the sky or the very air itself. He felt sure people would come to their senses and accept that truth before they did something really stupid, like fight a war that would tear this country asunder. As the crowd melted back into milling people Ray spotted his father coming out of the hotel. His steely hair glinted in the sun. Ray smiled. He had missed his father. They were very close. Ray's beautiful Apache mother had died giving birth to her first child. Ray became the one light of happiness in his father's life for many years after. People never saw one without the other. They were a small family, but a strong one.

Ray walked over to his father and they embraced unselfconsciously.

"Good to have you back, Son," Bill Michaels said patting Ray roughly on the back. His blue eyes shining.

"It's good to be back." Ray smiled down at his father. His father always said he had gotten his height and dark good looks from his mother.

"How did it go?" his father asked stepping back and looking up at him.

"Fine. I bought two bulls, white faced Herefords. They look like a couple of good breeders. Thought I'd see what kind of herd I could make of them."

Bill Michaels smiled with pride. He had put a lifetime into his ranch. It had become his main purpose in life, to build an empire for his son. He had raised his son to take his rightful place at its head when he died. But, so far, there were no signs of that. At fifty-five he was still young and vigorous.

"Did McGonigal give you any trouble over the price?

"None at all," Ray replied.

"Good, good," his father said, then drew his eyebrows together into a worried frown.

Ray looked closer at his father. Something's troubling him, he thought.

"Come on down to the ship and see 'em. Dan's unloading them now." Ray said.

"No, I'll see them later." His smile completely dropped away. "Let's go up to my room. I have something important to talk to you about." He and Ray walked into the hotel.

Up in the suite, a light breeze billowed the green velvet curtains hanging across the opened windows. Ray sat on the green brocade settee and stretched his long legs out in front of him. Ray looked uncomfortable sitting in the dainty gilded walnut furniture. He wondered how long the delicate furniture could hold his tall frame. He watched as his father poured two glasses of whiskey, handed one to him and took a long pull from the glass he kept for himself.

"A terrible thing happened while you were away," his father said still looking down at the amber liquid that remained in his glass. "Bessie Camden was kidnapped."

Ray was caught off guard. Of all the things he imagined could have gone wrong, this was not one of them. Bessie's image flashed through his mind. Sweet little thirteen-year old Bessie with the butterscotch hair and caramel eyes.

Now Ray understood why his father was so upset. Bessie was Senator Camden's only child. He and Brian had grown up together, as close as brothers," their neighbors in Virginia used to say. When Camden married, Bill Michaels moved away to The Oklahoma Territory to build his ranch. Brian Camden moved to Mississippi, built a prospering cotton plantation and became a United States Senator making him one of the most influential men in the south. Although they saw each other seldom over the years, they never lost their affection for one another and Brian Camden's tragedy was Bill Michaels tragedy as well.

Ray looked at his father intently and asked the first question that came to his mind.

"Why?"

"It's treachery, Son, pure treachery. There's been a rumor a group of men were trying to kill Brian so he hired a company named Pinkerton Investigations to send some men to work security for him. When Pinkerton's men infiltrated the assassin's group, they arrested the men hired to do the killing, they didn't know who hired them. It had been set up by a go between. They communicated through couriers, never the same one. After they were caught, Brian began to stop worrying and life returned to normal for a while.

Then one day Bessie didn't come home from school. Later that evening, a letter was found stuck to the front door with a knife. It said that if Brian will throw all his political influence behind Abraham Lincoln at the Republican Convention next month and at the elections in November, his daughter will be safely returned to him." His father looked grim. "Of course, I don't have to tell you what they'll do to Bessie if he doesn't cooperate."

Ray saw the Senator's dilemma. The people of Mississippi would not stand by peacefully and allow their Senator to support Lincoln. If he didn't, he could be sacrificing the life of his only child.

"So, what's he going to do?" Ray asked.

His father drained his glass and set it on the table.

"Right now, he is keeping a low profile, staying at home, pretending to go along with the kidnappers. But he hired Pinkerton's Agency to come in and see what they could find out."

"Have they learned anything yet?"

His father nodded.

"Two things. One, that Mr. Lincoln is positively not involved in this in any way, and two, that the men who are believed to have taken Bessie are hired hands on a ranch in the Texas Hill Country, just outside of Austin, owned by a rancher named John Weston."

"If they know that much, why don't they just go down there and get her?" Ray asked.

"Pinkerton feels that Bessie would be in greater danger if his company went any further with their investigation. He found out Bessie is still alive and probably will be kept alive until the general election in November. If the kidnappers thought anyone knew where she was, they might kill her instantly." His father's eyes narrowed. "These are powerful and dangerous men we're dealing with. If even a hint of what we know is given to the wrong people, it could cost Bessie her life. And we are not sure who the wrong people are."

Ray nodded slowly.

"What Pinkerton suggested," his father went on, "is that one man, uninvolved in politics and unconnected with him, who he could trust completely, go to the Weston Ranch and find out what is going on there. His sources have found out that the Weston's are going to Galveston to collect a young lady coming to visit and to hire on some new men. Camden's man could hire on as a ranch hand and be available to pick up on activities and

49

information but he would have to be very careful. If discovered, it could mean death to Bessie and possibly the man, too."

Bill Michaels looked square into his son's face. "Ray, the Senator feels his man is you."

Ray looked down at the yellowish dust that powered his black leather boots. He knew how much this meant to his father and all the people involved.

"When do I leave?" he said quietly.

Pride glowed warmly in Bill Michaels eyes. But what couldn't be seen below the glow of pride was a fatherly concern that would remain until his son returned home safely.

It was late and Ray was tired when he finally went to his room. He and his father had planned all afternoon and during dinner. Now that the plans were set Ray didn't want to think about it anymore. He just wanted to relax and let the worries of the day take care of themselves.

Someone knocked and he opened the door. A shapely blonde stood in the hallway.

"Mista' Michaels?" the girl asked in a slow southern drawl.

Ray looked her up and down. "Very pretty," he thought.

"My but you're handsome," she said. "Your friend said to tell you that Dan sent me."

Ray laughed then stopped and really looked at the girl standing before him. She smiled, but it seemed slightly forced. Her blue eyes sparkled but, he thought, probably not from some feelings about him but from some drink or drug she had consumed.

"What's the matter, Sugar. You don't like me?"

"I like you just fine," he said. Then taking some money out of his pocket, he said, "Here's enough money to get yourself a room here at the hotel. Take the night off. Have a nice dinner. Get a good night's sleep. In the morning, get on a horse and hightail it back home. Don't waste your life like this." The girl looked at him like he was crazy.

"Mister, I can't take your money for doing nothing."

"Take the money. You won't be doing nothing," he said. "You'll be safe and well fed. That's important to me. Do what I say."

The girl looked confused, but she took the money and hurried away.

Ray closed the door thinking about a green-eyed copper haired English beauty his body had craved since he last saw her. Then, he thought of Bessie out there somewhere waiting for him to find her. "Be safe," he whispered and headed for bed.

Chapter V

Cathy stepped slowly down the gang plank. Her face looked gaunt, her eyes glassy, her hands shook as she fidgeted self-consciously with the covered buttons on the front of her gray print dress. The six weeks on the ship had been a nightmare. After finding her ship on that awful night she ran straight to her cabin and locked the door. The dank room smelled of dead fish and puke and once out to sea, the ship had pitched constantly. Cathy kept to her room. She did not want any of the passengers to see her for fear they would read the shame in her eyes, or worse, recognize her as the girl who started the horrible fire in London. Thank God no one was hurt. She heard their accusing voices in her sleep.

"There she is. She's the one," they shouted in her dreams. Then she could see herself being thrown over the side to drown or shackled and returned to London—and the hangman.

Throughout the crossing, what little food she had been able to force down did not stay down long. And every knock at the door was a new terror, larger than the last, until she was even afraid to call out to ask who was there. The steward would just leave her tray of food outside her door. But when the ship made port in New York, a few days of relief from the pitching improved her appetite and as they skimmed the eastern coast of America, the weather became warmer, the seas quieter. When they finally sailed into the Gulf of Mexico, Cathy had regained most of her strength and rationality. The passengers no longer looked like demons, but like people, each involved in his or her own life, paying her no heed at all.

Now the fellow passengers passed her on the gang plank and ran to shore into the arms of waiting relatives and friends. Cathy paused to watch them.

"Catherine, Catherine Wilmershire?" The woman's voice came from a short distance away.

"Yes, I'm Catherine Wilmershire," Cathy called out.

"Over here, Dear, over here," a woman waving a white handkerchief called back. Cathy waved at her and made her way over to where the woman stood. She held her arms out to Clara. Clara put her arms around Cathy as tears started running down her face. So many times, in the past six weeks, Cathy thought she was going to die. But she hadn't. She had made it. She was safe. She laughed out loud and let the tears fall.

"My poor baby," Clara comforted. She lifted her white handkerchief and dabbed it at Cathy's eyes and nose. "This trip has been too hard on you, Child." Her voice was smooth and comforting. "I never travel by boat. That dreadful sea puts my stomach all out of countenance."

Cathy smiled at Clara holding firmly to her hand. "I'm sorry," Cathy said. "It does mine, too."

53

Clara laughed. "Well, it's over now. Let me make a proper introduction."

"As you know, I am Clara Weston and this is John Weston and we are so pleased to see you again after all these years."

"How do you do?" Cathy said looking each one in the eyes and making a quick curtsey. Clara was smaller than she remembered with a matronly figure. Her brown hair had begun to turn gray but she still had her pretty hazel eyes denoting a kind, caring attitude. John Was still handsome with blonde hair, wide shoulders and steely blue eyes.

"Thank you for allowing me to come and visit," Cathy said to them both.

"Not at all, not at all," Clara insisted. "We think the world of your brother Leonard. Why, you are practically family, especially now."

Cathy wondered what she meant by that but before she could say more, Clara released her hand and began giving orders.

Clara looked at John.

"Cathy's not feeling well. We should get her straight to the hotel." John nodded.

"You two go ahead to the wagon. I'll find the luggage and be right there."

"There's just the one trunk," Cathy called to him,

"One trunk! My goodness, Child, you travel light." "I don't have many gowns," Cathy said.

"Well, we'll soon fix that. I know of the loveliest shop over on Main Street. We will stay there for hours. It will be such fun."

54

Cathy let herself become lost in Clara's prattle and for the first time in years her heart felt light.

"One trunk. My Goodness. You know, my daughter Sylvia refuses to travel with less than four trunks. Sylvia and Peter will be so glad to see you. John and I were surprised to receive your letter telling us you were coming." She paused and looked at Cathy for a moment then continued. "We were sorry to hear of your father's passing. Sometimes being in a new place is exactly what a body needs to rejuvenate, refresh. Oh Catherine, I'm so glad you came."

Cathy had not expected the whirl of activities waiting for her in Galveston, Texas. After a couple of days of bed rest and regular meals, she was her old self again. The two weeks flew by with nonstop shopping, fittings, evenings at the Opera House and late dinners in expensive restaurants. Cathy felt dazzled by the social life she never had at home. In addition, Clara helped her arrange to have her inheritance in London deposited in a bank near the Weston Ranch. She had decided on the journey over that the first purchase she would make when her money transferred was a gun to protect herself. She had been so innocent that night she left home. She had no idea she could be stuffed in a bag and left in a brothel. She knew better now, and next time someone decided to try that again, she was going to be ready.

On the last night in town, as a special treat, John took them to spend an evening at the Palace Hotel, a gambling saloon notorious for its high stakes and rich patrons. Cathy dined on raw oysters and champagne and, after dinner lost every cent John had given her at the roulette wheel. But she wanted to lose, to throw her money carelessly on the board then laugh gaily as the croupier slid it away. She looked beautiful in the new gown. Ice blue satin held wide by the new crinoline, cut low in front with just the wisp of a corset cover between the bodice and her bare skin. Her face flushed from the champagne, the sparkle from the prisms on the crystal chandeliers flashed in her blue-green eyes and she felt young and alive, with her toes upon a precipice, like a champagne bubble about to pop. Every man in the room was hopelessly captivated and it was with the greatest reluctance that they bad her good night. But, as Clara told them, it was late and Cathy had to be up early the next morning to start the long journey home.

Morning came four hours before dawn. Forced from bed by Clara's persistent tapping on the door, Cathy pulled on her old gray gown and pinned her thick auburn hair up into the funny looking sun bonnet Clara had brought to her the night before.

"The road is going to be hot and bumpy," Clara told her, "so try to be as comfortable as you can."

Cathy did just that and after stumbling down the stairs, she crawled up into one of the four covered wagons they would be traveling in for the next twelve days and lay down on the pallet Clara had made for her.

"So, this is what a champagne head feels like," Cathy thought still a little tipsy from the night before, "sort of like looking at the world through tissue

56

paper. But what a wonderful night it had been." She nestled down into the warm blankets. "Gambling and flirting like some lady of quality." She paused. "No, more like a-a coquette, free to go where she pleased, to flirt and have fun." She giggled. "If she had really been a coquette last night which of the men in the saloon would she have chosen for her lover? Would it have been the fat rich one? All coquettes need a rich lover. Or would it have been the gallant who had kissed her hand and flirted outrageously. It is too hard a decision, "she sighed. "I would simply have to take them both."

She smiled to herself at her childish musings then her smile faded. The image of her lying in the center of that dirty, bug infested brothel rose vivid in her memory. Her light mood vanished and she rubbed her eyes trying to erase that image forever.

Cathy looked up to see Clara staring at her through the canvas slit at the back of the wagon. "Are you feeling unwell, Child. "You look about to cry," Clara said in obvious concern.

"No, ma'am," she said quickly removing her hands from her eyes. "Just sleepy." She smiled.

"The men are hitching up the teams now so we'll be leaving soon. It will be about an hour before we reach the mainland ferry. Why don't you try to get a little sleep, Dear?"

Yes, ma'am" Cathy said. She listened to Clara's footsteps as she walked away. Clara had been so kind to her.

"I wonder what Clara would think if she knew the truth about me, that I am not young and innocent anymore. What would Mother, the girls, Marcus and Leonard think of me now?"

That was too devastating to think about. No, that must never happen. No one would ever know, she swore. All that happened that night was between herself and God, her carnal sin, and she would take it with her to the grave.

Dawn broke as the small wagon train finished the ferry crossing from Galveston Island to the main land of Texas and started out on its journey to the Weston Ranch. The wagons jingled and jostled along the primitive rutted road and Cathy learned right away that she wasn't going to be able to travel in this manner for long. She would have to ride a horse astride, she decided. When Clara had insisted Cathy buy those strange skirts split up the middle, Cathy had hesitated but now she realized they were the wisest purchase she had made. They would allow her the freedom of riding in comfort.

It was the middle of April. The sun had already stoked its fire for the hot Texas summer. Cathy felt tired and gritty, groggy from the long ride. They camped at noon for lunch then traveled on until nightfall. Just when Cathy decided she could not take the jarring another minute, John gave the signal to camp for the night. The drivers pulled the four wagons in a semicircle. Cathy's wagon was first, the supply wagon second, the cook wagon next, and the Weston's wagons at the other end. When they finally stopped, Cathy jumped down to the ground. A cool damp breeze brushed across her face and she looked out over the flat land. There were no hills or trees to stager the skyline, only scrub brush and an occasional cactus. With the sun setting and the coolness coming on, the air smelled fresh, slightly salty, almost pleasant. Harnesses and tack jingled as the men unhitched the horses and readied them for the night. Cathy watched Slim Hopkins, the cook, as he gathered wood for his fire and piled it high in the center of the camp.

Taking a pan from the side of her wagon, Cathy walked over to the supply wagon and filled it with water from the large barrel strapped to the side. The water sloshed as she walked but she managed to get most of it back to her wagon. Placing it on the floor, she removed the sunbonnet and all of her clothes. The water felt cool as she splashed it over her body then dried off using one of the blankets for a towel. Somewhat refreshed, she took the pins from her hair and brushed it as hard as she could trying to loosen the accumulated dirt from her scalp. Her muscles felt sore and her joints began to stiffen. She realized from her first day as a Texan that life was hard in this wideopen country. She was going to have to grow stronger, be braver, learn self-sufficiency without fear and definitely without regret if she was going to be an independent woman in the great west of this country. Funny but instead of that thought being daunting, Cathy felt excited at the challenge and ready to start building her new life here in this great country, America.

She smelled food beginning to cook. She took her camisole from the hook where she had hung it and slipped her arms through the straps then quickly buttoned it. She pulled her faded gray dress over her head and secured the closings. In spite of the heat and perspiration, her hair curled nicely hanging loose down her back. She climbed down from the tall wagon deftly in bare feet and followed the lovely smell of food over to where Slim had built the campfire earlier.

John and Clara sat facing each other beside the fire. They looked to be involved in serious discourse. Cathy stepped lightly on her bare feet so as not to interrupt. As she drew closer, Cathy realized they were arguing. John's fair complexion held a crimson hue and the veins at his temples and sides of his neck stood out noticeably. Clara looked conciliatory but her efforts to sooth her husband did not seem to be having any effect.

"I still don't think we should have outsiders at the ranch right now," she heard John say.

"But she is not an outsider," Clara said. "She is Leonard's sister. Leonard feels she is best kept out of the way. He doesn't want her around when the transfer takes place. She is too inquisitive, he says. We can keep an eye on her here. No complications."

"What?" Cathy thought.

Just then, John and Clara looked up to see her approaching. They both smiled. Cathy smiled back.

"Come, join us, Dear. I bet you are starved."

"I'm afraid it's true," she said hoping they could not tell she had heard any of their conversation. "I

60

am not used to so much fresh air." She laughed. "My appetite has not yet adjusted."

John and Clara laughed with her and as far as she could tell, they did not suspect she had heard a word. When, in fact, she had. The idea that John was not happy with her presence made her feel extremely uncomfortable. But even more disconcerting was the knowledge that Leonard wanted her "out of the way."

"Here's some grub for ya', Miss." Cathy hadn't heard the cook, Slim, walk over to her. She looked up at him and smiled her appreciation taking the food gratefully.

"Thank you, kind sir," she said. He blushed and hurried away.

All during dinner she sat quietly trying to imagine what sort of business transaction would require her absence from home? Leonard wanted her here. He was up to something. Something he didn't want her to know about. And, knowing Leonard, whatever it was, she was much better off not knowing about it.

After dinner, Cathy moved closer to the warm fire and stared into the molten orange glow of the fragrant burning wood. The fire popped sending tiny glowing sparks in every direction like miniature fireworks. Cathy watched the burning ashes disappear up into the cool night air.

Slim Hopkins walked by gathering scattered dinner plates from off the ground. He stopped and smiled at Cathy.

"How do you like pork beans and biscuits, Miss?"

Cathy laughed and Slim was dazzled.

61

"They were delicious, the most delicious I've ever tasted," she said.

Slims chest swelled two inches.

"Thankee, Ma'am, thankee." He bobbed his head and beamed. John cleared his throat.

"Excuse me, Miss," he said stepping back almost tripping over the coffee pot which sat beside the fire then slipped off into the darkness.

Clara laughed. "I think you've made a friend, Dear."

Cathy couldn't help but laugh in agreement as she watched another man approach the fire but stop just outside the circle of light.

John picked up a tin cup and filled it with coffee then handed it to the man.

"You eat yet?" John asked him not sounding concerned, just making conversation.

"Yeah, thanks," the man said.

Suddenly Cathy sat up. Her whole body tensed becoming instantly aware of the new presence just a few feet from her. Trying not to look obvious, she glanced at the black outline of the man but he was just a vague shadow in the darkness. He drank the coffee and handed the cup back to John.

"More?" John said.

"No thanks. I have second watch tonight. I better save it for then. Evenin' Sir, Ladies." He rose and was gone.

Cathy couldn't move. "That man was familiar—frighteningly familiar," she thought. She could not see his face but his voice, his movements, his body. A shiver ran through her. She shook herself mentally.

"No, it couldn't be. Her memory was playing tricks on her. She was tired. It has been a hard day."

Suddenly feeling jumpy and restless, she stood and kissed Clara on the cheek.

"I'm a little tired. I think I'll go to bed," she said.

Clara sounded alarmed. "Why, you're shaking, Child. Are you ill?"

Cathy shook her head no. "Just tired," she said.

"Maybe I had better go with you to be sure," Clara said.

"No, really, I'm fine," Cathy said just wanting to get away and be alone. "All I need is some rest."

"Well, alright, Dear. Good night." Clara acquiesced but still sounded worried.

"Good night, Ma'am. Good night, Sir." Cathy dropped a small curtsy and walked back to her wagon. In the dim light from the whale oil lamp inside Cathy sat cross legged on the floor. It couldn't be him, she told herself. She was only with him for a short time. She probably wouldn't know him if she ever did see him, nor he her. Her shaking calmed and she turned down the light. She stretched out on the pallet.

From out of nowhere, a large hand clamped across her mouth and a long, hard body dropped over her. Without being able to see through the dark, she knew who it was. She lay completely still even though she could not move if she wanted to. His body was chipped granite against her.

"So, we meet again." Ray Michaels spoke. His breath hot on her face, his voice a threatening whisper. "Word has it you are coming to live with these nice people. Friends of your brother's." He didn't wait for an answer. "I'm sure they would be interested to know a story about a girl and her passionate night in a brothel."

Cathy tried to pull her face away from him but he held her tight.

"You wouldn't want them to hear that story, would you?"

Cathy did not move.

"I have a deal to offer," he said. He spoke slowly as if each word held an importance of its own. "If you keep your mouth shut about ever seeing me before, I'll do the same for you. But if you breathe one word
about me to your friends, I'll tell them in vivid detail how I came to know you."

Like a predatory beast he sensed her surrender. His body relaxed and he unclasped her mouth letting his hand slide down the side of her face to come to rest on her soft chest. She was as beautiful as he remembered. With a passion surprising them both, Ray covered her mouth with his and kissed her deeply, desperately as if she had been lost and he would never see her again.

"Get your hands off me!" she whispered as fiercely as she could in a whisper. Ray drew back far enough for Cathy to reach under the pallet for the gun she had bought in Galveston and dug it into his ribs.
"Right Now!"

Ray slowly rolled off of her.

Free from his weight, she quickly scrambled toward the front of the wagon. Her hands shook, her voice shook, but she gripped the gun with both hands pointed straight at his chest.

"Now I have a deal for you. You stole something from me that I can never get back. You raped me while I was drugged and couldn't protect myself." Ray sat perfectly still and listened to her.

"You leave me alone. Don't touch me, don't jump on me and I might continue to let you live. And don't you dare sneak in my wagon again! Now, get out of here."

Ray stared at her for a moment then nodded and crawled backward out of the wagon.

Cathy wasn't sure how long she held the gun pointed at the closed flap of the empty wagon, but as soon as her heartbeat slowed enough, she lay back down on the pallet. She turned onto her side bringing her legs tightly together and hugging the pistol close against her chest.

"What am I going to do?" she thought feeling as alone as the loneliest person in the world. "I could shoot myself," she thought looking at the gun, "but I'll have to buy some bullets." She shook her head at her own stupidity. "I guess I'm going to have to take shooting lessons."

In the darkness and quiet Cathy fought back the tears. She watched the back flap of the wagon. An occasional breeze lifted the flap and she could see a distant star gleaming determinedly down at her. She watched the star slowly fade until, in a riot of yellow and pink, dawn broke.

Chapter VI

Cathy climbed down from her wagon early the next morning dressed in one of the riding skirts Clara had bought for her and a long-sleeved shirt to protect her skin from the sun. She was able to catch Slim before he started cooking to ask him if there might be a horse she could ride today. He promised to look after packing up his chuckwagon. Just as he promised, he cleaned his area and hurried off to find Cathy a horse. He returned with a small sorrel mare with four white hooves and a white blaze across her muzzle. Cathy noticed how the pony kicked every few steps. Cathy knew nothing about horses but even she knew that didn't look right.

"Here she is," Slim beamed and held out the reins for Cathy to mount up. Cathy looked unsure so Slim lifted her onto the saddle and showed her how to take the reins.

"You ever rid afore?" he asked.

"Not much," she answered. "All I have to do is hang on," she thought, "how hard can that be?" "I'll

66

be fine," she told Slim who looked a little nervous. "I just need to get used to this horse."

Cathy nudged the mare gently with the heels of her leather, high top work boots. The sorrel pitched and shied nervously but refused to move.

"What's her name?" she called to Slim.

"Don't know as she has a name, Miss," Slim said.

Cathy thought a minute. "Fancy," she said. "Her name is Fancy. Thank you, Slim."

Slim blushed. "Ok, Miss. Gotta' go hitch up my rig afore I'm late. Mr. Weston don't abide late." He headed off toward the chuck wagon.

"Ok, Miss Fancy," Cathy spoke in a soft, soothing voice, "Let's go." But the mare just raised her nose into the air and shook her head as if trying to shake free of the reins. Cathy was contemplating her next move when Ray galloped passed her on a huge buckskin stallion then reigned him in to a slow walk a short distance in front of her. Fancy snorted and shook her head once more then settled into a slow even pace behind the buckskin, stepping daintily between the pebbles and dirt clods.

Cathy's spine stiffened at the sudden sight of Ray. She tried to look away from him, out across the countryside or up at the clear blue sky but her eyes kept wandering back to him. In the light of the sun, he looked just as he had that night in London, tall with a lean hard body and dark mysterious good

67

looks. The only difference was the mustache. It made him look sardonic, dangerous, more like he was wearing a disguise instead of a spontaneous outgrowth.

"Why doesn't he want anyone to know who he is? What is he running away from? Or toward?"

"What is wrong with me?" she chastised. "Why do I always need to know why? Maybe he's just here, like that tree or that cloud. Ignore him. When we get to the ranch, I'll probably never see him again. He will work and move on."

Still, she could not help but notice how he moved with an easy grace. She could tell by the way he handled the big buckskin that he was a man who had spent most of his life in a saddle. She took in his hard thighs, broad back and muscular arms. Muscular arms that held her captive the night before. A shudder ran through her as she remembered the kiss, at first hungry and demanding then gentle arousing a feeling inside her of … , her thoughts stopped abruptly.

"What am I thinking?" she asked herself. She lifted her gaze from his hands to his face. He had turned and was looking straight into her eyes. He wore a blank expression but just before he looked away, Cathy thought she saw his left eye wink. She flushed with anger, turned the mare around and prodded her to the back of the wagon train.

All the travelers were relieved to make camp that afternoon. As they neared the town of Austin the land began to rise and fall into low hills and an occasional mesquite dotted the landscape. Buzzard hawks circled overhead in search of tiny game that hid in underground burrows forged in the tall green Johnson grass that covered the reddish soil. They made camp beside a clear running stream and before dinner, the men stayed busy filling the canteens and barrels with fresh water.

After dinner, Clara asked Cathy if she would like to freshen up in the cool stream nearby.

"Yes," Cathy cried and ran to her wagon for a blanket and fresh set of clothes. She had learned something else important about travel on the trail today. No one in their right mind rides at the back of the wagon line. All the filth stirred up by the travelers in front swirls around in the air and lands on the travelers in the back. "Not tomorrow," she promised herself.

"If I have to have a pout, I'll have it at the front. Whoever doesn't like it can go to the back." One odd wink would never send her there again, she swore.

Cathy and Clara met back by the campfire and walked to a pleasant spot by the stream covered amply from view by a clump of oak trees. They each located a private enclave to undress. Cathy could hear the stream mumble and slosh as it moved swiftly around a slight curve where a large flat rock hung out over the bank. She quickly stripped down to her

69

bathing sheath. She hurried passed Clara on her way to the beckoning water and dove in. At first the water felt so cold it stung her skin but in a few breathless seconds her body adjusted and she set right to work scrubbing at her gritty scalp.

Clara was not so brave. She removed only her dress leaving on her petticoats and carefully waded into the water until it splashed against her ankles. She reached into the icy water and dribbled it sparingly on her bare arms and rubbed a cake of rose scented soap over her arms and chest.

After a few minutes, Cathy's shivering stopped. The freezing water turned into a balm for her sore muscles. She took the soap Clara held out to her and she could not get clean enough. She lathered her hair three times scrubbing as hard as she could then got out and dried and put on her clothes. Her waist length hair hung heavy down her back and she sat on the rock combing it with her fingers until it dried to a shiny curling mass. Cathy felt like a new person. Clara sat down beside her and they talked, enjoying the fresh cool breeze until the sun began to set behind the trees.

"We better get back," Clara said. Reluctantly, both women stood, gathered her things, and headed back toward the wagons. Clara saw John sitting by the campfire talking to some of the men there. "Join us at the campfire?" Clara said.

"No, thank you. It was a lovely evening. Thank you for showing me the stream. I think I'll call it a night." Cathy hugged Clara and walked slowly to her wagon.

After hanging her wet clothes on the outside to dry, she climbed inside and lit the one lamp that hung on a peg attached to the center support hoop holding up the canvass covering the top half of the wagon. The practice of hanging as many things as possible on the support rungs left a comfortable amount of floor space in which to function. This made the wagon an efficient yet comfortable form of travel. "But not for too long," Cathy thought. She changed into an old faded green dress that was too tight to wear anymore, but felt soft and perfect to use for sleeping. She laid down on her pallet and reached under the corner to be sure her gun was in place.

"What's this?" she pulled the gun out into the light. "This isn't my gun," she thought, confused. "This one is smaller." She looked at the cartridge. "And it has bullets in it."

She felt back under the pallet for her gun, but instead found a box of bullets. For a moment her mind went blank. She thought back to when she last saw her gun. "How could this happen? No one even knew I had a gun except for—oh no, HIM!" At first, she felt afraid knowing he had come back. Then anger overrode fear. She jumped up and started out of the wagon, then stopped.

"What good was going to come of her running out to find him like some crazy person waving a gun around and screaming?" She asked herself. "That

71

hadn't solved anything before and it wasn't going to solve anything now," she realized. She walked back over to the pallet and sat down to think. "He doesn't seem to want to hurt me," she thought. "Why would he trade out my old gun for a new one?" She took another look at the gun. This one was smaller and lighter, easier to hold in one hand. It was filled with ammunition, while hers was empty. And he kept kissing her although he hadn't seemed to plan to at first. He always looked almost as surprised as she was afterward. And the kisses! The kisses were of a kind that could be quite pleasant if a girl was in the mood to be kissed. No, she was going to have talk to him again. "Him," she thought. She didn't even know his name. "Well, it's time to find out." She stood, slipped on her walking flats, and headed out the wagon again, gun in hand, but with a more successful strategy in mind.

Not wanting to be seen, she stayed away from the campfire. She could make out small groups of men sitting out under the trees, talking, probably drinking. Then her eyes adjusted to the darkness. She saw a tall form sitting alone some ways away from the others, a large horse nearby. She walked in their direction.

Ray sat under the sagging mesquite chewing on the end of a blade of grass. His big buckskin grazed a short distance away. Ray sat up as Cathy approached and at the sight of those velvety brown eyes she almost turned and ran away. She clenched her teeth forcing herself to walk on.

The gentle scent of roses filled the air as she drew nearer. Ray stood and looked at her but did not step closer.

"Hello," Cathy said trying to sound if not friendly at least not angry.

"Hello," Ray said. "Won't you sit down?"

"No, thank you. But you feel free."

"Thank you," he said sitting back down. He caught sight of the gun in her hand. She did not hold it threateningly but she did not hide it either.

"My name is Catherine, Catherine Wilmershire. What is yours?"

"My name is Ray, Ray Michaels. Nice to meet you."

Cathy glanced down at him, then looked toward the campfire. No one seemed to notice them talking. "What is your horse's name?"

"I call him Buck."

"He's beautiful."

"Thank you." Ray smiled at her and her heart felt like it skipped a beat. She stood quietly for a moment then held up the gun by its handle. "Did you put this in my wagon?" "Yes, I did," he said.

She looked into his eyes. "Why?"

"I've been wanting to explain myself to you since the last time I saw you but I haven't had the opportunity."

Cathy blushed and looked down. "What about now?" She sat down across from him. She placed the gun in her lap. Cathy decided she wanted to hear what he had to say. They stared at each other for a few minutes Then Ray took both of her hands in his and he began.

"When I went into that bedroom that night, I was really drunk. My friend Dan and I had been drinking all day. When Dan wanted to finish off the night with a pretty woman, I agreed to go with him. I never intended to take a woman. But things got out of hand. I looked at you, your perfect body waiting for me, I lost all control. It was like a dream. We fit together like we were made for each other. The next morning, I realized by the way you were acting that something was terribly wrong. You obviously did not belong there. I wasn't going to leave you there. I left to demand the madam let you go or I would send for the law when the fire broke out and everyone was running in different directions. By the time I got back to the room you were gone. I looked for you but couldn't find you. I waited to see if you had been lost in the fire but thankfully no one was hurt. You had escaped and I had to be happy about that."

Cathy felt numb. She had never considered any of that. She was so caught up in her own fear she hadn't thought of anyone else.

Ray scooted over to sit beside Cathy.

"I should never have been there in the first place, especially being as drunk as I was. I'm truly sorry." He put his arm around her and hugged her. He had expected tears, but she just continued to stare at him. "So, you can shoot me now if you still want to."

Cathy looked at the gun in her lap then laughed. She handed the gun back to him.

"No," he said with a half-smile. "You are right. If you are out in the world alone, bad things can happen. You do need to protect yourself. I said I wanted to buy you a gift. Please take this and learn how to use it. I think Slim could teach you the ins and outs of the gun. Then all you have to do is practice."

"Now that said, there's something you are going to have to remember. I know you. I know your naked body, your silky hair, your secret yearnings when you're touched. If you ever want to know that part of that night, just come to me. I won't turn you down."

Ray stood and offered Cathy his hand. She let him pull her to her feet. He put the gun back into her hands, then to her surprise, he gently pressed his lips to hers. He cupped his hand under her chin and kissed her long and slow.

Her head swam and for a minute she thought she would faint. Then he suddenly released her. She stumbled but caught her balance just in time. She looked at his handsome face.

75

"Thank you for the explanation and the warning," she said in a low, silky voice she had never heard before. She cleared her throat. "Thank you for the revolver. I will talk to Slim tomorrow about lessons. Thank you for the advice. I'm sure some of it will be quite helpful someday. Good night," she said with a little curtsey.

"Good night." Ray said and watched as she strolled to her wagon and climbed in.

Ray smiled and unsaddled Buck. He untied his bed roll from his saddle and made a bed in the soft grass below the mesquite tree. He watched until the lamp in her wagon faded to a pale glow. He slipped blissfully to sleep.

So far, life in America agreed with Cathy. Her face became a golden tan. The fresh air and sunshine made her healthier every day. Her muscles became hard and strong from the continual riding. Most importantly, since she had spoken to Ray, the knot in her stomach had finally started to unwind. She felt more relaxed, more in control of her feelings again. She hated to admit to herself that knowing him as a person not an evil force in the world made the world a more balanced place. She needed to learn that all setbacks are not crises. They are learning points. Take what you need from it and move on, she thought.

The days passed quickly as the small wagon train skimmed the outskirts of Austin and traveled through rolling rocky land of the Texas Hill Country. Cathy noticed how the air became drier and the land less fertile as colonies of spikey green cactus became more common and valleys of lush grass less. Cathy decided to take advantage of the time on the trail and learn how to be a pioneer woman. Slim Hopkins was thrilled to have a pretty student. They began meeting for shooting lessons which consisted of gun safety practices, knowledge of gun maintenance, and practice, practice, practice. Slim also taught her the intricacies of preparing a filling if not tasty meal over an open fire. One night she cooked an entire meal all by herself and everyone seemed to enjoy it. At least no one complained. And every morning the men would gather and watch amusedly as she tugged and wrestled with her heavy saddle until she had it almost high enough when the prissy little mare would step aside and send it falling back to the ground and Cathy with it. She could tighten the stirrups and work the bridle into place but she just didn't have enough strength yet to lift the saddle. She found this frustrating. She had expressly told her audience to leave her alone. She was determined to do it herself. So, the men would stand back and enjoy watching her bend over and turn from side to side trying to get the saddle into place. Finally, one of them would come over and toss it easily onto the mare's back. The only one who never helped her was Ray. He would just lean back atop his big buckskin watch.

The group traveled on until finally in the early afternoon of the twelfth day they passed through the huge rock gates of the Weston Ranch. The yellow three-story house was quiet when they rode up to the front. "Siesta Time" Clara explained. But as they climbed the steps up to the wide wooden porch that surrounded the house, the ever-busy Maya, the Weston's housekeeper, ran out of the front door and hugged Clara fondly. Cathy had never seen a woman from Mexico before. She was fascinated by Maya's blue-black hair and beautiful dark eyes.

"Aye, Senora, it is good to have you back. I have missed you so much," Maya said to Clara and Cathy could tell from the look on her face she meant it.

"I missed you, too," Clara said smiling.

Maya dropped a short courtesy toward John.

"Welcome home, Señor."

John nodded in reply and followed the six men over to the bunkhouse to introduce the two new hands to the others and catch up on news of the ranch.

"Maya, this is Cathy," Clara said after watching John disappear into the bunkhouse.

"Buenos Días," she said smiling at Cathy. "But we can get better acquainted inside. Come. You are both in need of a good cool bath."

She swept them into the house like a mother with two small children. She hurried them up the winding staircase but Cathy had enough time to glimpse at the lovely entryway. It seemed large to her, larger than the parlor back home, with a copper chandelier hanging from the ten-foot ceiling and a soft cranberry carpet which covered the entire floor and ran up the stairs all the way to the top. A solid black walnut hat rack over six feet in height, Cathy judged, stood by the front door. A light oak tall-case clock with a painted wood face, mahogany top and shell inlay stood against the adjacent wall where it could be easily seen from what Cathy assumed was the parlor and two French style love seats sat along the opposite wall. Cathy longed to pause to examine each luxurious item more closely but by now Clara's small frame was half way up the stairs, talking rapidly. Not wanting to appear rude, Cathy followed along behind her chatting hostess to a bedroom on the second floor.

Clara turned to Cathy. "I'm afraid there is no sitting room," Clara apologized. "But this is the only empty room on this floor. Sylvia's room is over there," she pointed at the door at the end of the landing, her nurse has a room connecting to it and I am right over here," she indicated the room next to Cathy's.

"A nurse?" Cathy interrupted. "Is your daughter not well?"

"No," Clara answered. A concerned frown wrinkled her brow. "My daughter has never been strong, she was a sickly child at birth, but her health took a turn for the worse several years ago. She is somewhat improved now but we had to hire Miss

Pettigrew to keep constant watch over her lest she should fail again."

"I am so sorry, Clara. Please, I am a very good nurse. I cared for my father during his illness. I hope I may be of some help to you and Miss Sylvia during my stay in your beautiful home."

"You are a sweet girl," Clara said, "but Miss Pettigrew is very efficient. I prefer to leave Sylvia's care totally in her capable hands." She glanced at her daughter's door and frowned.

"Of course," Cathy said wondering what malady required constant watching.

"Besides, you are here for a vacation. One never works on one's vacation," Clara said in her normal chatty tone. "Now," she continued, "John and Peter share the rooms on the third floor so I couldn't very well put you up there." She laughed. "So this will have to do."

But when Cathy stepped through the door, she could not imagine why Clara would apologize for this. She had never seen such an elegant room. The floor was covered with the same rich cranberry carpet that covered the stairs and hall. The walls were papered in a pretty floral print design. All the dark mahogany furniture matched perfectly, from the three-drawer vanity to the huge oversized fourposter. Cathy walked over to the bed and pushed tentatively on the mattress. It was luxuriously soft. She could hardly wait to crawl beneath the white damask coverlet. A nimbus of white lace draped over the canopy and matching lace curtained the two floor-to-ceiling windows which led to a small private balcony outside.

"Do you think you can manage in this small room, Dear?" Clara asked.

Cathy couldn't help but laugh. She thought about her attic room back home with the bed barely wide enough for her slim body, the tiny dresser, the one candle for light, the little dormer window and the wooden chair with no two legs the same length.

She went to Clara and hugged her close.

"I shall manage just fine."

"Good," Clara replied. "I'm going to check on Sylvia and rest awhile You stay here and get settled. Maya will take good care of you. I will see you at dinner," she said closing the door behind her.

Cathy stood for a moment and stared at the door. Something about Clara had changed, she thought. The twinkle in her eye, the lightness in her step seemed to disappear as soon as she entered the house as if there were something she did not want to return to. Cathy shook her head and smiled at herself. That's silly. Why would Clara not want to return to this beautiful house?

She looked around the room once more. She was living in a palace and, she surmised, she was going to be very happy here.

A light tap sounded on the door.

"Come in," Cathy called out. Immediately, the room filled with young girls chattering away to one another in Spanish. They looked like miniature Mayas. Their full multicolored skirts and white peasant blouses seemed to be uniforms of the house and in their soft leather sandals, they moved through the halls as quietly as ghosts. One group carried in a large wooden tub and filled it with buckets of steaming water. Cathy tried to speak to one of the girls but evidently, she didn't understand English. She just smiled, nodded, and went on with her work.

In a flurry of hands, Cathy was bathed and dried and put to bed in a fluffy new nightgown. Within an hour, the bath things were cleared, the trunks unpacked and everything in the room put to perfect order.

Refreshed and relaxed, Cathy luxuriated in bed until one of the young house girls came in to help her dress for dinner.

"Which gown would you like to wear, Senorita?" the girl asked to Cathy's surprise. She had decided none of them spoke English. Cathy crossed to the wardrobe and looked inside. "I think the yellow," she said."

The girl took the dress off the hanger while Cathy stepped into the petticoats.

"Have you been here long?" Cathy asked her.

"Sí, two years," she said.

"Are you happy here?" Cathy said noticing the girl lower her dark eyes toward the floor as if reluctant to talk.

"Oh, sí, sí, Senorita. I hope I have done nothing to displease you."

"No, no," Cathy assured her. "I just wanted to get to know you." She raised her arms and the girl slipped the gown over her head. "To be honest," Cathy said pushing the gown into place around her waist. "I was hoping you could help me. I have not seen Sylvia and Peter Since they were children. I thought if you might tell me something about them, I wouldn't feel so nervous meeting them at dinner. What is your name?" "I am called Feliz as I am always happy to please, Senorita." The girl smiled prettily.

"What kind of person is Peter?" Cathy asked.

"The senior, he is a very nice man, smart," she pointed at her head. "He works hard on the ranch."

"What about Sylvia? Do you know about her illness?"

"Very little. I have heard that when she had thirteen years she became sick and could not eat. She got very skinny, so skinny La Senora sat with her every night for fear she would die and no one would be with her. They took her to the best doctors they could find and, slowly, she recovered. But, La

Senorita, she becomes ill very easy. You must see that she has everything she wants."

The girl finished fastening the dress and Cathy sat down at the vanity.

"Poor Sylvia," Cathy thought watching in the mirror as the girl brushed the loose snarls from Cathy's hair. "It must have been terrible for her. And lonely. Perhaps having a friend to talk to would help take her mind off her affliction." Cathy hoped so.

Feliz put one last pat to Cathy's hair and stepped back to admire her work. She had left the long auburn curls loose down Cathy's back and pulled the sides smooth and pinned them in a curling stream at the back of her head. Cathy owned no jewels. Realizing this, she slipped out of the room and returned

carrying a yellow ribbon which she tied around Cathy's long slender neck.

Cathy looked at herself in the mirror. The lemon yellow of the dress brought out the gentle peach of her tan and the willowy green in her blue-green eyes. But she felt unsure. Her nerves had turned to tiny crawling things inside her stomach. She wanted Sylvia and Peter to like her and she was almost afraid to meet them for fear they wouldn't. She looked herself in the eye. The time had come. She had made it this far. There was no turning back now. She took one daisy from the vase on the side table and walked down the grand staircase to the parlor.

The two men stood as Cathy entered.

"Catherine, don't you look pretty," Clara exclaimed coming over to Cathy and taking her by the hands.

"Peter, this is Catherine Wilmershire." Clara led Cathy to where Peter stood.

Cathy gave him a curtsey and a nervous smile. He was not tall for a man, she thought, less imposing than his father but he had the same thick curly blonde hair and cool blue eyes that marked all the Weston men. He looked to be in his mid-twenties, handsome but not ruggedly so, as Cathy expected, but stylishly so in the English tradition.

Peter shook her hand then continued to hold it while he looked her up and down then smiled in approval.

"And this is Sylvia," Clara said placing her hand at Cathy's elbow and guiding her to a large wing back chair opposite the sofa.

Sylvia stood and Cathy blinked twice in surprise. Where was the frail invalid she was so selflessly going to nurse back to health? She wondered. Surely this stunning creature before her was not the one.

"Hello," Sylvia said, her voice a breathy whisper.

Cathy hugged her lightly. "It is a pleasure to meet you."

Sylva stared at her through wide golden eyes. She looked to be around twenty with pale blonde hair that shined silver in the glow of the candle light. Her peaches and cream complexion held just the right amount of blush on each cheek. Her large frame, at least two inches taller than Cathy's, supported a full robust figure.

Odd, Cathy thought, Sylvia did not look like a person who had been suffering from a horrible illness for the past six years. Cathy remembered how rapidly disease had devoured her father's flesh leaving him weaker every day until, at the end, only wrinkled sallow skin covered his pointed bones. No, nothing about this young woman looked ill except her eyes, those wide staring eyes like those in need of strong guidance.

It must have taken years of practice to perfect that, Cathy thought, then stopped, shocked at her own rudeness. She looked at the daisy in her hand. How could she think such a terrible thing after Clara had been so kind and generous? Feeling ashamed, she handed the daisy to Sylvia.

"Dinner is ready. Señora," Maya's voice came from the doorway and taking Cathy's arm, Peter escorted her into the dining room.

Chapter VII

"Delicious as usual, Maya," Clara said as she preceded Cathy and Sylvia into the parlor. "I hope you will excuse the men, Catherine, but I don't allow their smelly old cigars in the parlor so they always retire to the study after dinner." She gestured for Cathy to sit on the deep purple sofa. She and Sylvia sat down on the matching chairs. The room was large but the furniture was bunched into several groups convenient for conversation making it seem cozy and intimate in spite of its size.

"Did you have a pleasant crossing?" Sylvia asked, her voice barely more than a whisper.

"Poor Catherine," Clara said, "was quite ill when she got off the ship. It was a very poor crossing, wasn't it, Dear?"

"Yes, I'm afraid it was," Cathy said shifting nervously in her seat. She did not want to discuss her trip or any of the events leading up to it.

"I became quite accustomed to riding every day on the trip here," she said looking at Sylvia. "I thought, if you would like to, we could go for a ride tomorrow morning and you could show me the ranch." Sylvia drew her perfectly arched brows together.

"As my mother probably told you, I am not well. My body cannot stand the strain of being bounced around on a horse. I am also very susceptible to heat stroke." She wet her full lips for emphasis. "But sometimes I do go for a ride in my buggy that Daddy had especially made for me. I suppose I could ride for a while after breakfast, before the sun becomes too hot."

Clara looked at her daughter.

"Darling, if you think it will be too much of a strain, Catherine will understand."

"I'm sure she would, Mother, but I said I would go," Sylvia snapped, wide eyes narrowed obstinately.

"Alright, Sweetheart, don't become overwrought. You know how hard it is for you to sleep when you become tense," Clara soothed. "This has been a trying day for you with our return and all. Come, let's go up to bed. I'll have Maya bring you a nice warm sleeping draught." After saying their good nights, they went upstairs leaving Cathy alone in the parlor.

As soon as the two left, Cathy rose from the sofa and strolled through the large open window onto the wide porch outside. She leaned against the railing and looked out across the short distance to where a yellow light glowed in the bunkhouse window. A refreshing coolness hung in the still evening air. A strange wistfulness engulfed her. The memory of a tender, demanding kiss, of her body responding to intimate touches took her back to a similar night sitting under a mesquite tree in thick, sweet-smelling grass. A soft voice in her ear.

"If you ever want to know that part of that night, just come to me."

"Hello. Where did everybody go?"

Cathy jumped and swung around to see Peter walking through the window. She knew he couldn't read her thoughts but she blushed just the same.

"They retired for the night," she said feeling completely flustered. She turned back to look at the night trying to regain her composure.

"Good," Peter said, "That gives us a chance to become acquainted." He leaned against the railing and studied her profile that shown silver against the moonlight. Her eyes held a dreamy glow and her lips were parted, soft and tempting as if inviting a kiss. He wanted to accept that invitation, she looked so lovely standing there. But it was too soon, he thought.

"What do you think of America so far?" he asked.

"Oh, it's beautiful," she said. "The climate is so warm and dry here, not like back home, when it rains at least twenty days out of the month and is foggy the other ten."

Peter laughed.

They talked on for nearly an hour about England, the ranch, and anything else they could think of then the high-case clock chimed in the distance and Peter stood upright.

"You must be exhausted," he apologized as if just now aware of the time. "I am just not used to having such charming company. I'm afraid I have kept you up too late."

Cathy didn't feel the least bit tired after resting all afternoon but not wanting to appear unladylike, she took the arm he offered her and allowed herself to be escorted back into the house. Back in the Parlor, he turned to her and lifted her slender hand to his lips.

"Thank you for a most enjoyable evening," he murmured against it. His breath tickled as he spoke. He stood, looked deeply into her eyes for a moment then turned and strolled out of the room.

Cathy stared after him until the slam of the front door broke the spell and she found herself standing in the middle of a totally silent house. She did not want to go to bed but with everyone else asleep or gone, there wasn't much else she could do. Slowly she walked to the stairs. Step by step she headed for her room pondering her new situation.

Catherine awoke early the next morning out of habit. She breakfasted in her room and dressed in one of her new riding skirts.

"I hope Sylvia is ready," she thought as she knocked lightly on Sylvia's door.

The door opened just a crack. The center half of two small black eyes and a very thin nose peered out at her. Sounds of heaving and retching came from inside.

"Miss Sylvia is under the weather," the nose said. "I am afraid having a stranger in the house has set her stomach aflutter." The half eyes narrowed and Cathy suddenly felt a wave of guilt wash over her. "But she has requested me to tell you that she will be down to ride as soon as she recovers from this seizure. Please wait downstairs."

The door shut firmly and there was nothing for Cathy to do but go downstairs and wait.

Maids ran to and fro carrying water and draughts and wet towels. Clara rushed by wringing her hands, not even noticing Cathy sitting on the bench in the entryway. It was about fifteen minutes, Cathy guessed, before the hustle and bustle calmed and Sylvia swept down the staircase resplendent in a pale pink gown, bonnet and parasol, each trimmed liberally in pale pink rosebuds. She was the picture of a spring garden with her nurse and maids buzzing around her like a swarm of hungry bees. They flew passed Cathy in a flurry.

Cathy stared at them in amazement then realizing she had let her mouth fall open, she clamped it shut, rose and followed along behind them.

Finally, after much ado, the ailing beauty perched daintily upon her buggy ready to go. Cathy walked up to the little red mare she rode on the journey here. As she swung up into the saddle, she made a decision that would become a major rule in her life, she thought. Riding with Sylvia was not going to be one of her daily activities.

All set, Sylvia instructed the stony-faced driver where she wanted to go and the sight seers were off. They saw the green hills and valleys, hundreds of cattle and herds of beautiful horses running free.

What are all these small houses?" Cathy asked as they rode along.

"Those are used by the hands," the driver answered. "Sometimes they have a job that takes several days. They can bunk out here. The houses are stocked with food and supplies. They don't have to waste time riding back and forth to the main bunkhouse. They can stay out here until they're finished."

Cathy laughed.

"This place is so big anyone could move into one of them and live for months. No one would even know they were there."

Sylvia stared at Cathy for a minute then turned to look out ahead.

They were approaching a group of ranch hands. Cathy could see they were busy working with the cattle. One in particular caught her eye. Ray stood over a low burning fire holding a tool of some kind. He held it against the hind end of a baby calf for a few seconds then let it go. The calf ran back to what Cathy assumed was its mother braying as if telling her a story. She looked back at Ray. Their gazes met and Cathy looked away immediately.

"Good morning, Ladies. This is an honor," Peter called as he rode over to where they were. He pulled up his horse beside Cathy's.

"You've probably never seen a calf branding before, have you, Catherine?"

"No, I haven't," Cathy said suddenly feeling selfconscious.

"If you care to ride over here with me, I'll be glad to explain how the process works."

"I would be most interested," she said wanting to put some space between herself and Ray.

They rode off toward an area where six or so men were rounding up cows and cutting out the calves into a separate group. Sylvia sat in her buggy. Her wide helpless eyes peered unwaveringly at the man working by the fire.

Ray released the calf and watched it run back to its mother. He looked up to find he had attracted the attention of the pretty young lady in the buggy. He smiled and removed his hat.

"Miss Weston," he said wiping the sweat from the band with a bandana from his back pocket. He wanted to talk to her but he knew her brother would consider that to be unacceptable for a ranch hand to stop work to flirt with his sister. He couldn't risk losing his job here right now. He replaced his hat, nodded politely and went back to work.

Sylvia lowered her pink parasol and leaned on it.

"You're new here, aren't you?" she called out to him.

"Ray stood up at looked at her again. "Yes, ma'am."

"Sometimes I have little jobs for the men to do. I will send for you should something arise," she said.

"I'm sure the pleasure would be all mine."

As Ray spoke, he looked over at Cathy. She smiled up into Peter's face as he was obviously saying something amusing. Cathy pressed her palms to her heat flushed cheeks and brushed a tendril of hair from her forehead. For a minute he wished that was him bantering with her, looking into those sensuous blue-green eyes. He looked back at Sylvia.

"I better get back to work, Ma'am," he said and nodding his head politely, he turned his attention to the branding iron and the task at hand.

With some effort, Cathy kept her gaze on Sylvia and Peter. "We had better get back to the house. Your mother will start to worry," she said to them both.

"I'll ride back with you. It's lunch time anyway," Peter said.

The riding party headed for the house at a leisurely pace.

"I sure hope she has that gun," Ray thought listening to the sound of her voice in his head fade away into the noon day's heat.

Chapter VIII

Clara, John, and Peter Weston sat talking in the parlor when Cathy came down for dinner that evening.

"But Peter, Dear" Clara said," it's time you settled down, started a family, got serious about the ranch."

"This girl is right for you for many reasons," his father said.

"Maybe, but…" Peter stopped mid-sentence. Three wide-eyed faces turned to look at Cathy at once.

She stopped just inside the doorway. The pale blue gown she had changed into set her complexion aglow. Peter moved first taking her hand and escorted her to the sofa. He had just poured her a glass of Sangria when Sylvia entered. Her pale green dress trimmed in cream colored lace showed her blonde beauty to perfection. She sank exhaustedly into the nearest chair. Her mother rushed to her side.

"Are you feeling alright, Dear?" Clara asked.

"I am a trifle weary from that grueling ride this morning." She looked at Cathy. "I think that after dinner I shall just go straight up to my room."

Peter looked at his sister and smiled to himself. He had seen her talking to that new hand this morning.

Dinner was delicious again and afterwards Sylvia went up to her room as she promised. Cathy and Clara went into the parlor and sat down on the velvet sofa.

Clara clasped her hands in her lap and looked at Cathy lovingly.

"John and I have been talking." She sounded hesitant. "We would like to introduce you to our friends."

She smiled at Cathy and Cathy smiled back.

"The best way to do that would be to give a party in your honor." She spoke a little faster now. "We could have an afternoon barbecue with a formal dance to follow that evening. It would be so much fun. We could show you off in style. What do you think?"

Cathy's eyes lit up. "That would be wonderful!" she exclaimed. She had been to very few parties and none had been in her honor.

Clara looked pleased.

"All right then, I'll make all the arrangements for a week from this Saturday."

Clara chattered on about new gowns and decorations and refreshments. "Does that sound agreeable to you?"

Cathy couldn't think of a more generous family than the Westons. "Clara, this is so exciting. Everything sounds wonderful. Please let me help with the work. I know parties are fun but they require a tremendous amount of work."

"No, I won't hear of it. You just show up looking as beautiful as you are. I'll handle the rest."

Cathy stood and kissed Clara on the cheek. "You are too kind, Clara. Your family has taken me in and made me feel like a member. How will I ever repay your kindness?"

Clara laughed. "We'll think of something, My Dear."

Cathy laughed and kissed Clara again. "Thank you. I will see you in the morning." She ran up to her room.

To her relief, the room was empty. She shut the door behind her and locked it. It was all very elegant to have maids dress you, Cathy assumed, but she was accustomed to seeing to herself. The busy girls made her nervous, uneasy. Her room had always been a retreat for physical privacy as well as private thoughts.
And, Cathy decided, she much preferred it that way.

She undressed slowly, taking care to hang each petticoat just so in the big mahogany wardrobe. There was little for her to do in her spotless room and she was grateful for the activity.

With the clothes put away, she slipped on her soft white nightgown and sat down at the vanity. The three tortoiseshell pins slid out of her hair easily. The beautifully crafted nest of soft ginger curls cascaded past her shoulders to her waist like a shimmering waterfall. She brushed at it absently wondering how she should arrange it for the party when a sudden movement in the mirror caught her eye. Her arms froze in mid-motion and her heart pounded against her chest as she stared through the lace curtains at the black outline of a man. Then he stepped into the light and fear gave way to exasperation.

"I thought we were in agreement. You are not going to sneak into my room anymore."

Ray crossed the room in three long strides and grabbed her by the wrists. She tried to throw the brush at him, but it just fell to the floor with a muted clunk..

"Quiet. I just came to warn you."

"About what?" she said.

"About this." Ray released her hands and gently brushing the curls from her face, looked longingly at her luscious breasts silhouetted against her sheer cotton gown.

"Be careful when you go out riding. In fact, it would be best if you don't go out alone at all."

"Be careful of what?" she asked, surprised. "What could happen to her here?" she thought.

But Ray didn't answer. "And be more careful about leaving your windows open at night. Anyone could get in here without any trouble at all."

Cathy smiled and shook her head in faked weariness.

"The only person I have to worry about is you."

Ray laughed a low sensuous laugh.

"Do you still have your gun?" he asked.

"Yes," she said. "Why? Just tell me. What's going on?"

"I'm telling you what I know. Watch out for the boss's son. He's not a nice person."

"What does that mean?" she demanded looking deeply into his eyes for an explanation.

"Just trust me," he whispered slowly walking toward her. She backed away until the cold wooden side board on the bed pressed flat against her calves. With one hand, he reached out and twisted his fingers in the hair at the back of her neck. She looked around desperately but it was no use. She couldn't move. He slid his other arm around her slender waist and tilted her head until the only thing in the world she could see was his handsome face.

He spoke low and quiet now and Cathy shut her eyes against the passion in his voice.

"You were right that night when you said you needed to protect yourself. I am going to help you do that."

He bent over and kissed her with the same slow kiss she had thought about so many times since that night under the mesquite tree. Then he drew back and his soft lips moved lightly over her mouth as he gently lowered her back onto her bed. The thin nightgown did nothing to hide her body's response to his touches. He continued to kiss her letting his hands move over her body. Her breathing quickened and she felt dizzy. The room was spinning around them. Cathy sighed. A strange need started to grow inside her. Then his voice, breathy and strained, whispered in her ear. "I have to go now. Good night my beautiful Cathy."

"Go? Her foggy brain screamed but before she could try to stop him, he left through the same windows he had entered, closing them behind him.

"What just happened?" she thought looking at herself, the bed, the room around her, the closed window. Had she fallen down the rabbit hole? she wondered trying to clear her head. She didn't want to make sense out of what just happened and her reaction to it. She wanted to know why she had to watch out for Peter? He's not a nice person? Something odd is going on around here, she thought. And how did she get in the middle of it?

The next morning, Cathy's eyes popped open with a start. The bright morning sun streamed through the opened windows. She climbed out of bed, closed and locked the windows, then washed and dressed for her morning ride. No one was about so she found some bread from last night's dinner and made a cup of hot chocolate then carried them to the front porch to eat. The sun felt warm and relaxing. After eating, she made her way over to the stables and saddled Fancy. But even the invigorating gallop along the open countryside failed to distract her from the questions stuck in her mind from last night.

"Catherine," someone called her name. She looked up to see Peter riding toward her.

"Good morning," he said pulling his black stallion up in front of her.

"Hello," she said.

"I was just going to see if the branding was finished."

"Would you mind if I came along?" she asked.

"I would love it."

As they rode side by side, Cathy glanced over at Peter. He was quite handsome, she thought. He seemed like such a gentleman.

Peter looked over at her noticing the distracted look in her blue-green eyes and the frown wrinkling her brow.

"Is the sun too warm for you, Catherine."

Cathy smiled brightly. He was so considerate.

"Not at all," she replied and heeled Fancy into a leisurely canter.

Chapter IX

Ray stood and brushed the circles of dirt off his pant legs. A drop of sweat rolled down his eyebrow and dropped to the corner of his eye. He tilted his hat to the back of his head and wiped his face on his sleeve. Mid-morning, he thought squinting up at the sun. It had been a long time since he had gotten up before dawn and mended fences but he hadn't been able to sleep. He scooped up a handful of dirt and watched as the multi shaped grains sifted through his tanned fingers. If he could put the constant thought of that green-eyed vixen out of his head for at least one minute, he might be able to think clearer. Even when she wasn't around, her voice whispered in his ear arousing everything masculine within him. And those lips, perfect for kissing, made him want to kiss her until she throbbed for the feel of him. He rubbed his hands together absently.

"What am I going to do with her?" he thought. "I need to find Bessie Camden and get her home safely. But is Cathy going to be safe after I'm gone?" Just

104

the thought of leaving her here felt impossible at this moment.

Another drop of sweat rolled down his temple and he flipped it away with one finger.

"Why am I standing out here thinking when I know what I have to do."

Wasting no more time, he unhitched Buck, swung up in the saddle and headed out.

Over the past two days he had ridden across a great deal of the ranch with no results. There was no talk of Bessie in the bunkhouse, no clue to her whereabouts at all. If she was somewhere on this ranch, she was well hidden. She was going to be hard to find. And finding her wasn't the most difficult part. How was he going to get her away without getting both of them killed?

The questions ran through his mind as he rode along for the next hour, searching all outlying buildings along the way. The cabins were stocked with jerky and water, even straw mattresses but none showed signs of being recently used.

This is useless, Ray thought about to give up when he came to the top of a hill. Below, sheltered on three sides by hills and partially hidden by a group of trees sat a house, larger than the others he had seen today with three horses tied outside. Ray dismounted and tied Buck in a clump of bushes.

He approached the house slowly, careful not to be seen. Familiar voices floated out through an open window and he drew nearer.

"How much longer we goin' to have to sit out here?" one voice said. It was familiar but Ray couldn't quite place it.

"Not much. They'll be shippin' her in two weeks. We can get our money and be done with the whole thing then," another voice Ray had never heard before said.

"You in a hurry to get back to fence mending, Amigo? Guarding the chica too hard for you?"
"Shut up, Sanchez."

The unmistakable click of a gun being cocked momentarily silenced the group.

"Maybe you will shut up, Amigo."

"Both of you shut up," the unfamiliar voice said. "Sanchez, put that gun away. I'm not havin' any trouble here. Not after we come this far. In two weeks, they're gonna ship that little girl off to England and we'll finally get paid. After that, you two hair-brained idiots can go blow each other's heads off but until then you're gonna both shut up."

The gun clicked again as Sanchez released the hammer.

"Two more weeks. Is she gonna stay quiet that long?"

106

"Sure. Just keep putting them powders in her food and water and you'll never hear a peep out of her. She'll sleep like that all the way to Galveston. Then she'll be somebody else's problem."

Someone grunted in reply and Ray moved back away from the window.

Was that Bessie they were talking about? Ray wondered. He had to find out for sure. Carefully, he walked around to the back of the house until he came to another window. This one was closed. Very slowly, he stood up and peeked inside. He saw a closed door and what at first sight appeared to be an empty room but it was hard to see through the glare on the window pane.

Ray cupped his hands around his eyes and looked closer. There in the corner, on a dirty yellow quilt lay Bessie Camden. He could see the rise and fall of her chest. She appeared to be in a very deep sleep. Ray felt relief and dread at the same time. He tried to open the window but it wouldn't budge. He couldn't chance breaking in and shooting his way in was out of the question. But getting in was not the hardest part. Getting out was the problem. He couldn't do anything stupid. He was going to have to make a plan and he was going to have to do it fast. In two weeks, they were sending her to England. She would be almost impossible to find there. Ray looked around making a mental note of possible entrances and exits to the house then backed away from the house into the bushes and disappeared up the hill.

Chapter X

"You in or out?"

Ray stared at the two deuces in his hand then folded and threw them on the table.

"Out."

He leaned back in his chair stretching his long legs out in front of him. It had been an hour past dark when he had finally gotten back to the bunkhouse and dinner was already on the table. Only two other men had come in after him, Raul Sanchez and Jonas Grey. He'd already known Raul Sanchez was one of the men at the cabin but he hadn't been sure of Jonas Grey until they had walked in together. But the third voice. He knew he hadn't heard it before and it didn't match anyone in the bunkhouse tonight.

"Hey, Lover Boy, I heard you are the new stud around here. Miss Sylvia wants to go riding tomorrow. Word is she wants you to do the riding." Hank Ledbetter's voice came from across the room.

Ray didn't look up.

"What I hear she already has a permanent rider and it isn't me or you. Some gun slinger, not open to sharing. You looking to start some trouble, Hank?"

Snickers came from around the room. Hank's baiting slipped to a hollow grin.

Ray looked at Hank as though he would yawn and deciding it would take too much effort, he shrugged.

"Truth is, Hank, I don't give a damn about any socalled gun slinger or his wandering slut. None of my business, none of yours either."

The room fell silent. Everyone stopped and stared at the two men. Hank cleared his throat and looked down at the floor.

"I was just havin' a little joke," he said.

Ray nodded but didn't smile.

The man sitting next to Ray picked up the cards and pointed at Ray.

"Another hand?"

"Naw, deal me out," he said rising from the chair. He crossed to the door and stepped out into the cool fresh air.

"Nat Callaway," he thought pulling a small cigar from his pocket. He lit it and flipped the match into the air. "Could this be the unidentified third voice from the cabin where he found Bessie? Miss Sylvia might know."

He strolled past the front drive and across the distance to the main house. Almost every door and window stood wide to take advantage of the cool evening and yellow light shone through every one. The bushes rustled as intermittent breezes wandered through them. Ray approached the front of the house, paused, then stepped back into the shadows. The sound of a soft feminine voice came from the porch. In the dark, he could make out Cathy's slender form. She stood against the railing. Her creamcolored gown glowed in the moonlight.

Images of Cathy's body, silky and pliant under his hands, played through his mind and without thinking, he glanced up at the closed window of her room.

"You truly are beautiful, Catherine. I so much enjoyed being with you today," Peter said. He stepped closer to her and took both hands in his. "I hope we will have many more days together." He kissed each hand then gently encircled her in his arms and kissed her lips.

Every muscle in Ray's body tensed. A warm flush heated his face and neck. He started toward the porch, then stopped. He watched as Cathy drew away from Peter and looked back out at the stars. Peter followed behind her and placed his hands on her shoulders. She moved away again. Ray yanked the cigar from between his clenched teeth and threw it on the ground. There was nothing he could do, he

110

thought looking at Cathy, wanting her in his arms, feeling her body against his body, feeling helpless. The image of Bessie lying asleep and in imminent danger, out there in that filthy cabin alone, wiped out all thoughts but one.

"I have a job to do, and this isn't it. I warned her," he thought, a sense of loss and regret already growing inside him. Unable to take anymore, he backed off and strode away.

For the next few days, Ray found himself with little spare time. House workers and ranch hands alike were constantly at a run polishing, cooking, cleaning, making everything ready for the big party scheduled for Saturday. Every family in the county had been invited and as far as Clara Weston knew, everyone was coming. Monday was mostly a cleaning day. Tuesday, all linens were washed and aired in preparation for overnighters and Wednesday, the huge pit was dug out at the side of the house, big enough to accommodate an entire beef carcass, two full grown hogs, and innumerable chickens.

Ray spent all day digging and filling the pit with mesquite branches. He had not been back to check on Bessie and he had still not thought of a way to get her off the Weston Ranch and back home to Oklahoma safely. He had no way of sending a message to his father and he was acutely aware that time was running out. He had just finished with the pit and started for the bunkhouse when Carl Johnson rode up.

"We're goin' into town. Wanna come along? Could be fun."

Ray appreciated the offer but the sweat and dirt had mixed together and collected in the folds of his skin. All he could think of was washing up and settling down in his bunk for a few hours rest.

"Naw," he said.

Carl waved a finger at him and swung his horse around.

"Suit yourself," he said and rode back toward the group of men waiting in front of the bunkhouse.

Ray washed out back then ate beans with pork belly alone. It was quiet for a change. Ray opened all the windows to let in the evening's coolness and lay down on his bunk. He tried to sleep but even though he lay in a shadow, the flickering lamplight tapped against his eyelids. Too tired to get up and turn them down, he reached out for his hat and set it gently over his face.

Just then the door banged open and Raul Sanchez and Jonas Grey staggered into the room. Obviously drunk, each plopped unsteadily into a chair at the table.

Jonas spoke first.

"Well, Amigo, it's almost payday. They'll be sending that young 'un off next week. What'er you goin' to do with your share?" He turned his head and sent a large ball of dun colored spittle splattering onto the floor.

I'm going to buy the fanciest set of clothes I can find and go get drunk. How about you?"

Raul's accent sounded heavier than usual.

Jonas grinned showing what was left of his brown teeth and rubbed his hand across his whiskered chin.

I got my eye on a fancy girl just my style. I think I will persuade her to come away with me for a few days. I'll keep her until all the new wares off, then find somebody to take her off my hands, for a price, of course."

They both laughed a hard, cruel laugh.

"Quen es?" he asked. Who is it?"

"It's that new piece of fluff old Pete has taken up with. If I know him, he's goin' to turn her over to us when he gets tired of her anyway. I just want to be sure I get first go at her."

"I heard he was figuring on marrying her, part of a deal him and her brother are figuring on. Her brother is going to buy some senator's spread in Oklahoma. They're going to marry off the girl to Peter and join both spreads together. That would give them all the water rights from here to the Red River. A lot of money for water with the cattle trails coming through."

"That's what Daddy is saying, Amigo, but you know Peter and his promises." Both men laughed.

"That's where I come in," Jonas said still laughing. "He'll do what Daddy says. He'll marry her, then she'll mysteriously disappear. Ain't no one'll care where she got off to. She's nothin' but baggage after that."

They laughed again, stood and slapped each other on the back.

"Let's go find the boys. They went to town. I done worked up a thirst."

Their laughter faded as they lurched and staggered out into the night.

A deadly silence fell over the bunkhouse. All movement in the room stopped, even the unrhythmic flickering of the kerosene lamps. Slowly, Ray raised his hand to his hat and pushed it back off his face. Feeling the strength of the Apache sun god his mother named him for, Ray dropped his feet to the floor and climbed out of his bunk. He took his gun belt down from its nail where it hung on the bed post and buckled it around his waist. The cartridge clicked rapidly—six times in succession—as Ray checked to be sure it was loaded then slid it back into the holster. Heavy lids hung lazily over usually brown eyes that now burned an ominous black.

Ray walked out of the door in the same direction as the two men who had just left.

114

Chapter XI

Cathy shielded her face from the eye watering glare of the early morning sun and hopped out of bed. Her bare feet sunk into the velvety carpet as she felt her way to the water basin. Taking a wash cloth from under the wash stand, she soaked her face in the cold water. The cold rag felt refreshing against her tender eyelids and she let it rest there for a few minutes before finishing. In the vanity mirror she could see her eyes slightly swollen, a red nose and two red cheekbones. Cathy sat down.

Too much sun, she thought. Clara had warned her not to overdo. But it had been such fun riding with Peter every day. She picked up the brush and pulled it through her hair. He was so handsome and such a gentleman. He paid her compliments and treated her like a lady. He kissed her gently on the lips, not hard and demanding, sucking the very life out of her until the world was a blur and the only feeling left was her need for him. Cathy's heart beat faster as she could almost feel Ray's hands on her.

"No, Peter," she thought but only the image of Ray's tender kisses left her breathless. She lowered the hairbrush to the vanity and sat motionless for a moment as the realization set in. She wanted him. He had said that if she wanted to know the rest of what happened that night in the brothel, he would be happy to show her. God help her. She really wanted to know.

"Mr. Weston!" the man's alarmed voice came through the opened window.

Cathy jumped up and hurried over careful not to be seen.

One of the ranch hands ran up to the house, his face flushed red.

"Mr. Weston," he called again.

John stepped out on the porch just beneath her veranda.

"What is it, Jake?" John Weston said sounding slightly put out by the intrusion on his breakfast.

"I didn't mean to disturb you, Sir, but some fellas just found Jonas Grey dead about two miles down the road. He's been shot. Straight through the heart."

A knock sounded at the door and Cathy jumped. Not wanting to be caught eavesdropping, she carefully closed the window and returned to the vanity.

"Come in," she called picking up the hair brush again. Maya entered carrying a cup of hot chocolate and handed it to Cathy. She took it gratefully.

"Jonas Grey," Cathy said to herself trying to remember his face.

"Come," Maya said taking the brush from her hands. "I will fix your hair."

Just then, one of the house girls ran into the room speaking loudly to Maya and waving her hands in the air.

"Calm down. Speak English," Maya said to her in a soothing voice. "What is wrong?"

"Someone shot Jonas through the heart last night on the road to town," she said gulping air and rubbing her arms as if trying to ward-off a chill.

"Aye," Maya said lifting her hand toward the ceiling.

"Who was he?" Cathy said.

"He was a ranch hand for Senor Weston," Maya said. "He was a pretty bad hombre. I was always careful never to be alone when he was around."

She shook her head.

"The news of his death does not surprise me. He was probably cheating at cards or messing with another man's girl. The important thing is not that he is dead but that there might be a killer on the ranch.

She shook her head again.

"It would be smart if you do not go riding today, Senorita. It is very dangerous out there."

Cathy looked back into the mirror. Another voice, Ray's voice, echoed the very same words in her mind. Was Ray involved in this somehow? she thought. Something was definitely going on here. Something bad.

Cathy's suspicions weighed heavily on her mind as she worked through the busy day. House guests began arriving as soon as she came down for breakfast and suddenly, she was thrust into the role of hostess. She greeted guests and assisted Clara see to everyone's needs. Sylvia helped very little. Pleading sick, she stayed in her room only coming down to greet the occasional friend who just happened to have a handsome brother or father. Once, Beatrice Gerhart and her ten children caught her by the stairs but a convenient swoon overtook her and she had to be assisted back to her room.

Cathy found her work a little hectic but exciting. And it was nice to see Clara so happy. She introduced Cathy to every person who came through the door. She proudly told them how Cathy had come from England. By the time Clara finished the introduction, Cathy sounded practically like nobility. She could never tell Clara the true sordid details of how she came to be here. If she did, she would have to leave. Clara didn't deserve the censure that would follow if the true story was known. Clara was so proud of her. How could she disappoint her like that?

Dinner went pleasantly for the guests as did the rest of the evening. Peter hovered close to Cathy most of the time and Sylvia stayed downstairs for a while. She sat in one of the winged back chairs with the younger men gathered around her. Fortunately, the guests wanted to retire early. That suited Cathy. She managed to remove her shoes and gown before her head hit the pillow and sleep overtook her immediately.

A few hours later, Cathy's eyes popped open with a start. A chill brushed across her bare arms and realizing she had fallen asleep in her petticoat, she climbed out of bed and let the petticoat fall to the floor.

"I'll pick it up later," she thought and climbed under the covers. A clicking sound, like the wind rattling the windows, or the door, she thought. Before she could rouse herself again, the noise stopped and she did not stir until morning.

Friday passed much as Thursday. Guests arrived as Clara dashed from room to room in a continual flutter. Cathy followed for about an hour then realizing there was too much to do, she left Clara to her fun and sat down to relax and enjoy watching the excitement. That evening, Maya served a large dinner in the dining room with card games in the parlor afterwards.

Cathy managed to slip away early. She felt a little guilty for not staying to help Clara but everyone seemed to be occupied with the games and she didn't know how to play cards. Besides, she wanted to be rested and ready for the ball tomorrow night. A thrill of excitement ran through her. It was going to be such fun!

Unable to help herself, she went to the wardrobe in her room for the hundredth time and took out the new ball gown. It was the most beautiful gown ever made, she thought holding it up to her body. The stark white satin shimmered in the firelight as she looked in the mirror and turned from side to side. The bodice was cut in an off the shoulders style with tiny puffed sleeves on each arm and yards of material draped around the skirt in a scalloped pattern caught up by small yellow rosebuds. The skirt stood full and with her crinoline on swung and swirled saucily showing glimpses of her yellow satin slippers.

She carefully returned the gown to the wardrobe and readied herself for bed.

She really should be downstairs, she thought crawling under the covers, her long chestnut hair spreading over the pillow as she lay down. But the thought of the ball being only one day away was just too exciting. She was going to laugh and flirt and dance all night long. It was going to be her night and she was going to make the most of it.

120

Chapter XII

Cathy eased down into the old tin wash tub and let the liquid heat close over her. But even the relaxing warmth of the water did little to relieve the tension in her body. Already the mariachi music floated through her window and the monotonous drone of chattering voices rose as guests began to gather outside. It had taken all morning to get the tub up to her room and filled. There were so many other chores to be done in preparation for the picnic and ball tonight. And now that she finally had her bath, she had no intention of sitting around waiting to be dressed.

The strong scent of roses filled the room as Cathy lathered herself with perfumed soap and she scrubbed her hair twice, soaping it good, making sure it would shine extra clean tonight. Finished with the bath, she dried herself with the big soft towel that had been left on her bed. She slipped on a fresh camisole and petticoat and sat down at the vanity to let her hair dry. It still felt damp when she brushed it

121

and pinned back the sides but she could not wait any longer. The picnic had started and she was ready to go now.

She had already decided to wear the dark blue muslin with the white print flowers and the blue kid slippers but finding the matching bonnet too confining, she removed a sprig of the white artificial flowers and tossed the hat on the vanity.

"That's not half bad," she said to herself pinning the flowers in the back of her hair. Taking one last look in the mirror, she whirled around and hurried out the door.

Outside, the smell of cooking meat drew Cathy to the pit where huge spits rotated with a cow, a pig, a goat and at least ten chickens. She watched the house girls dressed in their full red skirts and dainty white peasant blouses brush a spicy red sauce over the meat until it dripped onto the smoldering mesquite and sizzled to a poignant black smoke. It smelled delicious.

Suddenly ravenous, Cathy walked the few feet to where four large tables held more food than she believed could ever be eaten. Roasted corn ears, potatoes in every form, tangy baked beans, fresh bread with plenty of thick creamy butter in addition to all the delicious dishes from Mexico, refried beans, tamales, beef enchiladas bubbling in hot cheese, chicken enchiladas with sour cream and green peppers, piping hot sopapillas rolled in sugar and dipped in fresh sweet honey and cakes and pies of every description crowded together in mingling aromas to tempt her beyond control. Taking a plate, she filled it with everything she could squeeze on it vowing to return until she had tasted every delicious dish on the table. Lost in thought, she had not seen the man standing beside her. She turned and bumped right into him.

"Pardon me," she said. "I was in such a hurry to get away with this wonderful food, I wasn't watching where I was going." She smiled and looked up and the smile froze on her face.

"Certainly ma'am.' Ray tipped his hat and smiled back at her. He picked up a plate and started filling it. "Looks good," he continued, in a casual tone as if they were casual acquaintances. "Care to join me under that tree?"

Cathy didn't know what to say. She felt silly standing there, her hands full of food." There you are!" Peter called from behind them. "I've been looking everywhere for you."

Cathy quickly looked down at the ground as Peter came up, took her by the arm and led her away.

"We have a table set up over here."

Cathy followed along hoping Peter couldn't feel the pounding of her heart through her arm and a feeling of disappointment came over her. What would have happened if Peter had not come up when he did? she wondered and her pulse raced that much more. Was Ray disappointed too? She wanted so

123

badly to turn around and read the expression on Ray's face but Peter would see if she did. He would know they had been talking. He might even start to question her about Ray. No, that would never do. Besides, she told herself, she really shouldn't care what Ray was thinking.

"Here, let me take that for you," Peter said taking the plate out of her hands.

Peter introduced Cathy to the fellow diners already seated and eating.

"How do you do?" Cathy said to each one.

"Catherine is fresh from England," Peter said. "You know, they raise mostly Herefords in England. Do you have any on your ranch, Carl?"

"No, we don't. But I have talked to some fellas who do." Cathy picked at the food she had taken so enthusiastically only a few minutes before. It tasted good but suddenly she wasn't so hungry.

There must be at least a hundred people here, Cathy thought looking around at the guests. She spotted John and Clara sitting side by side visiting with Beatrice Gerhart and her husband Henry. Beatrice was laughing as usual. Cathy had liked her right away. It was hard to imagine someone who is happy all of the time, Cathy thought, but like Beatrice said, "With ten young ones you have to have a sense of humor."

124

She let her gaze wander over to the house and saw Sylvia on the porch. Her pink tulle dress cool as it fluttered around her. She appeared to be looking for someone, found him and walked down the steps skirting the crowd until she came to the large oak directly across the party from Cathy. Cathy watched with interest now as Sylvia squatted down beside Ray and put her hand familiarly on his shoulder. They talked. Sylvia seemed to be asking him something and he shook his head no. Sylvia leaned against him and started to raise her arms around his neck but he caught her hands and pushed them back down into her lap.

Cathy's eyes narrowed.

Sylvia said something else. She seemed to Cathy to be pouting. Ray stood pulling Sylvia with him. Cathy watched them walk off together, back toward the house.

Cathy stared at them, lost in her thoughts.

"Isn't that what you think, Catherine?"

Cathy turned to look at Peter. "What? Oh, yes, quite." She smiled and turned her attention back to her meal.

However, that odd scene between Sylvia and Ray nagged Cathy all afternoon. What exactly did that mean? Was Sylvia caught up in whatever is going on here? She kept asking herself but the answer seemed just out of her reach. She needed to find out more of what was happening on this ranch.

The afternoon passed pleasantly for most. The younger people organized games and the older people enjoyed sitting back and watching them play. Cathy managed to beat Peter at croquet. Cathy and even Sylvia joined in, flirting and in the center of fascinated men. But although she would never admit it, every once in a while, Cathy scanned the crowd for a face that was not there. After disappearing with Sylvia earlier, a low-grade depression left her feeling restless, tired and like she would like to be alone.

The feeling persisted long into the night. Even the compliments on her new gown and hair that Maya had so carefully pinned into lustrous flame tinged curls did not help. The sight of Sylvia, beautiful in her sheer silver gown, her pale blonde hair intertwined into a diamond tiara and the Weston diamonds at her throat and ears made Cathy feel even worse. From the first waltz Peter had not let her out of his sight. He stood close to her letting his hands brush against her arm or shoulder as they talked. When they danced, he whispered in her ear.

"I wish we were alone. Let's slip away. No one will notice."

His whiskey breath made her want to pull away but he held her hard against him, crushing her breasts against his chest, kissing her neck until she felt stifled beyond control.

"Peter, please, I must rest," she implored him several times but he just laughed.

"We can rest tomorrow," he said and pulled her out onto the dance floor again.

Champagne flowed and the guests became more boisterous and Peter pursued her until Cathy thought she would scream.

Finally, during a lull in the music, Henry Gerhart asked Cathy to dance and refused to allow Peter to put him off.

"Oh, come on, Pete. You've had her all night." The short, stout man had obviously been drinking all day.

Eager to escape Peter, Cathy followed Henry onto the dance floor but her respite was short lived. The drunk little man flung her most ungracefully around the dance floor until she feared for the safety of her teeth.

"O, my," Cathy said coming to a halt in the middle of the dance. "Please, Mr. Gerhart, would you get me a glass of champagne?"

He looked confused for a moment but she smiled sweetly letting her long thick lashes flutter just a trifle and he dashed off to do as she asked. She watched him weave his way across the room then headed for the nearest open door.

The cool damp air felt good and Cathy could feel her taut nerves relax. Freedom at last, she thought looking out across the front drive. The orchestra finished its waltz inside and the haunting melody of an old Mexican ballad played in the distance. Cathy listened to the hypnotic strum of the guitar as it seemed to create into music the strange sadness that she found impossible to put into words. The soft strains beckoned her like a kindred spirit and she followed, down off the porch a short way from the house into a clearing. There young house girls sat with ranch hands talking and enjoying the music. Cathy stopped and stood back in the shadows. She didn't want to intrude on their party.

Colored lanterns hung over the area on strings and the mariachi band that had strolled around and entertained the guests earlier now sat in chairs with their bright red cummerbunds draped over their chair backs and their starched white shirts open down the front playing softly in the background. Cathy looked around and her eyes came to rest on a face, the face she had been seeking all day.

Ray sat with a group of men laughing and talking. He smiled flashing straight white teeth, and his dark features showed relaxed and unthreatening through the darkness. He wore snug fitting black trousers and vest over a white lawn shirt, unbuttoned at the throat. He looked so handsome, Cathy thought, like a great handsome beast relaxed and happy in his play.

He leaned forward intent on the conversation around him then he raised his head and looked around as if suddenly aware of a new scent in the air. Cathy watched as he scanned the trees. She sunk back as his gaze seemed to bore in through the shadows straight at her then moved away and he fell back into conversation with his companions.

Had he seen her? she wondered slowly peeking out at him again but he showed no sign of it and she decided not feeling sure she was too well hidden.

From her secure nest of trees, Cathy continued to watch the sleepy party. One of the girls who had been sitting on the ground, stood and began to dance. The soft music grew louder and faster sending the dancer jumping and spinning until she strained to keep up with the wild beat. One by one the girls began to jump up to join in. The men watched yelling encouragements and clapping their hands. The girls stamped their feet and waved their arms in the air until the tempo became too fast and they started to spin sending their skirts high above their waists. Bare legs and feet flashed in the lantern light. Cathy watched intrigued as the music changed rapidly back to a very slow tempo and the dancers moved gracefully lifting their skirts and rotating their hips suggestively.

One beautiful girl left the others and danced over to Ray. She moved her hips from side to side and pursed her wet lips looking at him through half closed eyes. Then the music changed again becoming faster and faster. The girl kept perfect time with her feet as she twirled and moved in front of Ray, sometimes moving so close she hit him with her skirts. She danced harder and harder and, Cathy thought, she would surely die from sheer exhaustion when the music came to a complete halt and to Cathy's amazement the girl dropped into Ray's lap and kissed him lingeringly on the mouth.

Ray pulled her arms from around his neck and laughed down into her face.

"You better go find Naldo, Chica. I fear he has gone to find a gun to shoot me with. I sure don't want him to come back to hurt me. Besides, you are way too much woman for me."

This brought roars of laughter from the men. With a pout, the girl jumped off his knee and started to stomp away when one of the men reached out and slapped her solidly on the backside. Her fiery black eyes narrowed furiously and she turned and spit right in his face. This brought even louder laughter as the man jumped up and chased the squealing girl out into the darkness.

Cathy laughed too and moved on strolling toward the bunkhouse. The house girls were lucky to be so free, she thought. What would Ray have done if she had brushed out her hair and pulled off her shoes and danced barefoot in front of him? Would he have pulled her arms from around his neck and sent her on her way? She wondered but to her surprise she knew. He would not send her away, she realized and a pleasant thrill shot through her body.

She walked along at a leisurely pace but voices from behind sent her scurrying to the nearest tree.

"This way. Come on," a male voice muttered drunkenly. They stumbled by one man leaning heavily against the other for support.

She watched them walk in the direction of the bunkhouse. Not wanting to travel too far from the main house, she decided to turn back when the lit end of a cigar caught her eye. Through the trees she could see one of the ranch hands standing in the doorway of the bunkhouse. A man she recognized as one of Clara's guests walked out tying his tie with his evening coat hanging over his arm. He handed the man something.

"Is that enough, Raul?"

"Si, gracious."

Her curiosity aroused Cathy leaned back against a tree to watch.

Soon another man came out and two more came and left. Then a woman appeared from inside and Raul stopped her at the door.

"I am only going to take a rest. Give me a cigar." She was one of the older house workers, one of the cooks, Cathy thought.

Raul lit a small brown cigar and handed it to her. "Don't take long. It is starting to get busy."

The woman walked off and Raul went inside.

"So, there you are!" the voice sounded very close by and before Cathy could move, the puffy round face of Henry Gerhart blocked her field of vision.

"Mr. Gerhart, I-I was just taking a walk," she stuttered in surprise.

He wavered unsteadily and took a step toward her.

"A little walk. Huh?"

'Y-Yes, Sir."

He leered at her and weaved closer until he stood so close Cathy could not move without touching him. She looked around nervously. The tone of his voice was beginning to scare her.

"Don't be scared," he said leaning forward. A strange look glazed over his bloodshot eyes. He reached out and ran his fingertips across the tops of her breasts where they swelled alluringly above her gown. His breath blew hot onto her face. His wet drunken lips drooled like a mad dog's. He slid his hands over her shoulders and down her arms pushing the bodice of her dress lower, forcing it down against her breasts until the strong satin cut her skin. Cathy was sure the dress would rip asunder.

Then in a blur the overpowering weight lifted and she stood free staring at the frightened drunk lying spread eagle on the ground. Ray stood over him, the blue-gray barrel of Ray's gun pressed flush against his head.

Cathy jumped forward and put her hand on Ray's shoulder.

"He's just drunk. He doesn't know what he's doing," she said. "I'm alright." She straightened her gown.

Ray looked at her then back at Henry. He holstered his gun and lifted the shaking man to his feet.

"I suggest you go back inside," Ray said around clenched teeth.

Henry didn't hesitate. He ran back to the house as fast as his legs would carry him.

Still shaking, Cathy ran to Ray and threw her arms around his neck. At first his body felt taut with anger then she felt him relax as his strong arms encircled her. What was she doing? She thought but for the moment she didn't care. She was in a warm familiar place and she was safe.

Ray put his hand under her chin and tilted her head up to look at him. Misty green eyes sparkled in the moonlight and his mouth moved over hers ever so gently, he knew at that moment she wanted him every bit as much as he wanted her. He kissed her deeply with all the tenderness and longing he felt inside and Cathy kissed him back. She knew she should stop, pull away, but she couldn't. She was lost to him and there wasn't anything she could do about it.

Finally, his lips released her and she stepped back away from him, a contemplative look he could not read covered her face.

She stared at him and he just stood there, hands at his sides, his big brown eyes soft as velvet, his luscious arousing lips waiting.

Thoughts and feelings moved over face like waves to a shore. Emotions and confusion tumbled with them.

He stood there and watched the changing expressions dance across her face. He wanted her to run to him, to put her arms around his neck just as she had before. She was his now. She was his just as if he had taken her out and put his brand on her. But he couldn't force her. She would have to come to him now of her own will. He waited but she turned away and walked to where the mariachi music still played. He waited a few minutes then followed.

Cathy sat down on a bench under a tree where she could see the dancers. A young house boy walked by and she stopped him.

"Please go to the house and bring me a glass of champagne."

The boy ran off in the direction of the house.

Ray returned to the chair he occupied earlier.

The house boy ran up to Cathy and handed her a gaily colored bottle and a glass.

"Gracias," she said and poured out a glassful of the bubbling liquid. Raising the glass in a gesture of salute she nodded at Ray and drained it in one gulp.

Ray smiled at her and tipped his hat.

"You are in a barrel of trouble my girl," she mumbled under her breath and poured another glass of champagne.

After the third glass, she set the bottle beside her on the bench.

This is really quite refreshing, she thought looking at the empty glass in her hand. She glanced at Ray again. He sat tipped back in his chair, his arms crossed on his chest and smiled amusedly back at her.

"What am I going to do about you?" she mumbled and poured another glassful. It certainly was a warm night, she thought fanning herself with her hand.

A beautiful dark-haired girl danced past her. She poured another drink. The music seemed to be growing louder and the dancers whirling faster.

"If it wasn't for this cumbersome gown, I would join them," she thought and feeling slightly unsteady she put her legs up across the bench and leaned back against the tree. The empty champagne bottle hit the ground with a hollow thunk. In one graceful motion she downed the last drink and set the glass beside it.

"Catherine, I've been looking for you."

The voice floated through her fog and she looked up to see Peter standing in front of her. Not him, she thought giving him a crooked smile.

"What on earth are you doing here?" he asked.

"Getting some fresh air, but I couldn't resist the beautiful music so I stopped to listen for a while."

Peter raised one eyebrow and cocked his head as if trying to figure out a puzzle. Then he spotted the empty champagne bottle and glass. His pale eyes widened and a delighted smile crept across his mouth.

"Why you little minx," he thought. "You really shouldn't be out here unescorted," he said. "It is very late. I had better walk you back to your room." He bent down to take her hand.

Cathy felt a sudden panic. The tone of his voice and the glint in his eye made her hesitate. She looked across to where Ray had been sitting only to see an empty chair. Looking back at Peter, she allowed him to take her hand and help her to her feet. She needed all of her concentration to place her feet squarely, one after the other, on the constantly shifting ground. They had almost reached the house when a man Cathy had never seen before stepped out of some bushes.

"Sorry to bother you, Pete but I have to talk to you right away," he said nodding at Cathy.

Peter continued to walk toward the house.

"Not now, Nat."

"But it's about that cargo we're takin' out next week. It's important I talk to you about it right away," he insisted.

Peter sounded annoyed. "All right, wait for me in the barn." He turned to Cathy and took both of her hands in his. He spoke to her like someone would talk to a very young child.

"Go on up to your room but leave the door unlocked. I may be a while but I'll come up later to see that you got in safely." He released her hands and walked off in the direction of the barn.

Cathy exhaled slowly in relief.

"Ray, were you looking for me?" Sylvia said from somewhere nearby.

Cathy turned in the direction of the voice but saw no one. She hurried for the house.

An iron grip clamped down on Sylvia's arm and pulled her behind a tree.

"Stop," she yelped. "You are hurting me!"

Ray released her and her golden eyes softened as she pushed her full weight against him.

"Don't look at me like that. You know how ill I have been since you have stopped coming to ride with me. I can't eat a bite of food and I won't until you promise to ride with me again."

She stuck out her lower lip and tears formed at the corners of her eyes.

Ray glanced over to where Cathy was standing. Thank goodness she was gone, hopefully to the back entrance of the house.

"Look, Sylvia," Ray said pushing her away from him, "I can't make it any clearer. Your father and brother would probably shoot me if they could see me talking to you right now! This arrangement you want between us is a losing proposition. Ranch hands do not mess with the rancher's daughter. Now get back to your party before you're missed."

He nudged her toward the front of the house.

Her face popped out into a full pout. "You'll be sorry for this." She gathered her full skirt and headed for the front of the house.

Ray watched her for a minute then hurried to the barn. As he drew close, he could hear Peter and the other man talking.

"What's the trouble, Nat?" Peter asked.

"It's the girl. I think she's dead." Nat Calloway sounded worried.

Ray froze and a terrible dread came over him.

Peter sounded furious.

"Dead! What happened?"

"Nothing happened. She just stopped breathing."

"Someone probably gave her too much sleeping powder. I told you to be careful. Serious consequences will come of this and I am holding you responsible. Are you sure she's dead?"

"I think so."

"You think so! Come on, let's get back out there. I want to see what's going on."

Ray stood flat against the side of the barn to be out of sight when two rode off. He waited until they were out of sight then mounted the first saddled horse and heeled him into a gallop.

Sylvia stepped out of the shadows and watched him ride away in the same direction as her brother and Nat then strolled back to the house to join the party.

Cathy slipped up the back stairs and into her room. Even though her clothes seemed dead set against it, she changed into her nightgown, climbed into bed and drifted off into a champagne slumber.

The clock chimed three as Ray came silently into the room. He locked the door and walked over to the bed. She looked so innocent in that modest white gown, he thought, and knelt down beside her. Tenderly, he brushed a web of ginger hair back out of her face. Footsteps sounded in the hall then stopped. An impatient hand rattled the door knob.

"Catherine, are you awake? It's me, Peter. Open the door." He knocked softly and tried the door again.

"Damn," he swore then footsteps faded away down the hall.

Ray snickered and turned around to see two sleepy blue-green eyes staring straight at him. He sat back on his heels.

"Don't worry, I just came in to see if you were alright."

Cathy nodded her head sleepily and squinted up at him. "You are in my room again," she said.

Ray stood and smiled down at her. But it wasn't his usual smile, Cathy thought. It was teasing and warm. For some reason it made her feel good.

They watched each other for a minute, then reluctantly Ray walked over to the window and climbed out.

Cathy laid back on her pillow feeling safe and content and went back to sleep.

Chapter XIII

Cathy awoke slowly the next morning. A dull ache pounded just behind her left eye and she felt sluggish, slightly dull around the edges. She washed, coiled her hair on top of her head and dressed in her brown riding skirt and pale green silk blouse. No one was about downstairs and Cathy knew why, she thought rubbing the ache in her left temple.

Food was not a problem. Pounds of it lay all about the kitchen. Cathy wrapped a piece of cold chicken and two generous slices of fresh-made bread in a white napkin. Then she brewed a cup of strong tea and carried it out to the porch. The hot tea felt like a panacea to her hangover. Encouraged, she knotted the napkin to secure her breakfast and walked to the stable to saddle Fancy.

The solitude cleared her head as she rode across the dew-covered land, watching the mist sparkle in the breaking dawn light, allowing Fancy to wander as aimlessly as her thoughts. She felt like a princess in a fairy tale, riding her palfrey, surveying her husband's kingdom, dreaming about a handsome prince.

"But," she thought coming back down to earth, "this is not Camelot. Fancy is not my horse, I am not marrying Peter, Ray is no Lancelot, and this is no fairy tale. The Weston's, for whatever reason, have been very kind and generous to me. But it is time to go. I need to build a real life for myself. I need to find employment, a place to live, a community to join. This has been exciting, a champagne fantasy come true but the fantasy is over and I need to find my way to that path to a real happiness."

For the first time since that first night she was abducted and raped in that brothel, she felt like herself, stronger and more centered. She tightened the reins and pointed Fancy in the direction of the house. In the distance she saw one of the out houses. As they drew nearer, she recognized Sylvia's buggy and Buck standing outside. Fancy trotted up beside the big Buckskin and stood docile while Cathy loosely tied the reins to the post.

The door of the cabin stood ajar so Cathy pushed it open and walked in. For an instant she couldn't see but someone on the bed moved and she could clearly see two people locked in embrace. Then Sylvia raised her head.

"What do you want?" she shouted.

"Where's Ray?" Cathy said looking around the room.

142

The man started to get out of the bed.

"Who is Ray?" he demanded turning to look at Sylvia.

Cathy blushed crimson to her bones.

"I-I'm sorry." I saw his horse—" she spun around and ran out of the cabin.

"I have to tell Clara about this," Cathy thought jumping onto Fancy's back. "Clara has to know this is going on. But it will break her heart."

Dirt and grass flew out behind them as Fancy ran across the countryside heading for home. Sensing Cathy's urgency the pony galloped as fast as she could. They slid to a halt in front of the house. Cathy jumped down and ran inside. She heard Clara's voice coming from the dining room. She started toward the dining room then caught a glimpse of herself in the hall mirror.

Her hair looked fiery red as it stood on end around her face and her eyes flashed a bright green.

"I can't go in like this," she thought. Clara will think I've gone mad. She'll not believe a single word I say."

She slowed her breathing to a more normal rhythm then took down her hair and smoothed it as best she could with her fingers. Good enough, she thought looking at herself one more time in the mirror. But then John Weston's angry voice rang out from the room. Cathy approached the doorway carefully close enough to hear the conversation and not be seen.

"How could you be so stupid as to let someone follow you, much less listen to what you say? Who is this man? Where does he come from? How much does he know? Has he told anyone else what he has heard?"

Peter answered him in a soothing tone.

"I am finding all that out now. Sheriff Mitchell knows how to get answers from people who are, shall we say, uncooperative. It's about time that fat sheriff did something to earn all that money we pay him."

"Just the same," Clara said and, Cathy thought, she sounded as though she had been crying. "That was very sloppy of you both to let that ranch hand follow you around, Peter. Thank goodness Sylvia was paying attention or we would all be sitting in jail right now! John, you should have checked this man's background better before you let him come here and you, Peter, should have taken precautions against this sort of thing. You both have been very careless."

"Yes, Mother, I understand your point," Peter said in exasperation, "but I swear to you I can handle this. I'm sure he's just a two-bit cowboy from Oklahoma looking for a way to make some money. He thought by following me around he could get some goods on me to use for blackmail just as he said when we questioned him last night."

Could that be true? Cathy thought.

144

"There's nothing for us to worry about. The good sheriff will persuade him to tell all, then tonight he will be killed making an escape. No Problem."

Did he say killed!? Cathy thought.

John spoke up again sounding somewhat calmed.

"So, you have this man, what is his name?" "Ray,"

Peter said.

"You have this man, Ray, down at the sheriff's office safely locked up and you will get rid of him tonight. But make this a lesson. Don't let it happen again."

Outside the room, Cathy closed her eyes and let her head drop back against the wall.

Ray, she thought trying to make sense out of what she just heard. They are planning to kill Ray? But why? Why would they want to kill a man for following them around?

Unless they were doing something they did not want him to see. Something so terrible they would kill to keep it secret. No, there was something bad going on at this ranch. She had felt so for some time now. But she could only understand if she heard the rest of the story from Ray.

She straightened and started toward the front door when she heard Clara's voice behind her.

"Going for your morning ride, Dear?" she asked sweetly.

"Yes," Cathy answered trying to sound composed.

"Enjoy yourself."

"Thank you," Cathy said over her shoulder and hurried out the door.

Outside, Fancy stood nipping at the ground for any tender sprouts of fresh grass she could find.

Cathy gathered the reins and swung up into the saddle. She held Fancy to her normal morning ride speed until they were out of view from the house, then heeled her into a relaxed gallop so as not to draw attention. She found the main road to town easily. Peter had pointed it out many times when on their sightseeing rides. She did not know how long it took to get there.

Fancy galloped for nearly an hour before Cathy began to see signs of a town. She passed several houses, shop keeper's homes, she thought, then the road gradually widened into one long main street. A row of wooden buildings stood on each side of the street with a wooden walkway running the length of both.

What a parched looking sight, she thought pulling Fancy into a slow walk. No lamp posts, no shrubbery of any kind, no carriages dashing about on daily errands. Just a dusty rutted dirt street and a few wooden buildings with four or five sleepy eyed horses tied outside.

"Must be lunch time," Cathy thought.

She rode on passed the general store, saloon and barber shop then came to a shop with a sign that read Sheriff's Office. Cathy dismounted and secured Fancy then went up to the door. She glanced around nervously. What if someone from the ranch saw her going in? Would they ride back and tell Peter? Would they kill her, too?

"Good questions all," she thought, "but not the most important. The most important question is am I going to stand by and let them kill Ray?"

Without further hesitation, she opened the door and entered the office. A desk and chair stood in the middle of the room with an old cot in the corner and a barred door just opposite from where she stood. She closed the office door and finding the office empty crossed over to the barred door. A thick bolt secured it but she unlatched the bolt easily and pushed the door open.

A strange smell sort of like burning meat only worse drifted up to her nostrils. She jerked back but a sound stopped her drawing her closer to an area sectioned off into small cages. At first, she didn't see him then he moaned louder this time pulling her gaze to the floor. Ray was curled up in the corner, hands and legs tied together, clothes in rags. Cathy dropped to her knees straining to reach him through the bars.

147

She could see him clearly now. Dried blood peeled from his face and arms. Large red whelps swelled across his back. In some places, his skin looked as if it had been burned off. She could see a stringy pink substance with something white beneath.

"Oh my God," Cathy whispered.

At the sound of her voice Ray stirred. His red swollen eyes opened slowly and a glaze of pain sparkled on their surface. He stared at Cathy as if she were a hallucination then felt her touch.

"Cathy, is that you?" he managed through dry cracked lips.

"Yes," she said relieved to hear him speak.

"Quick, before they come back, I have to tell you something very important."

Steeling herself, she leaned on her elbows and pressed against the cold bars as hard as she could.

"Listen carefully, this means life or death to a child."

Cathy nodded her head.

"You know my horse, Buck? Take him and the saddle to the livery stable here in town and sell them to the owner there. His name is Tom. He'll give you one hundred dollars. Take that money and buy a ticket on the next coach to Hatten, Oklahoma. Check in to the Hatten House Hotel and tell the bell boy to ride out to the Michaels place and tell Bill that a messenger from Ray is waiting for him. He will come right away. Tell him this. The Weston Ranch in Texas, Peter Weston. He'll understand and see that you are cared for. Don't let anyone see you go and don't let on to anyone at the ranch you ever knew me in any way. Do you understand?" He looked at her, his face distorted with pain.

She nodded her head yes.

Seeing this, Ray relaxed and let his eyes close.

Cathy jumped up and ran out careful to close the doors behind her. Quickly, she mounted Fancy and trotted her slowly out of town in case anyone was around. Once out of sight of the town, she heeled the mare into an open run and headed back to the ranch. The sound of running hoofs drummed a rhythm like a ticking clock and she tried to think rational thoughts.

She had two problems. One problem was Ray's plan. She couldn't sell Buck. That friend of Sylvia's had him. And the second problem was that she was not going anywhere until Ray was safe. She had to get him out of that jail.

The ride back flew by in a blur but by the time she pulled up to the stable, she had a loose outline of a plan. She unsaddled Fancy, gave her a quick rub down and stole up to her room. She pulled the clean sheets from her bed, folded them into a pillowcase and replaced the bed spread as if nothing had been disturbed. Then she went to the medicine cabinet and gathered all the antiseptic, salve and liniment she could find and put them in the pillowcase. She sneaked down to the study, took a full bottle of whisky from John's private stock and put it with the other things. Finding the bunk house empty, she lifted Ray's saddlebags packed with all his possessions including a clean set of clothes and finally, as she passed the storehouse on her way back to her room, she took a slab of bacon and a bag of dried beans and packed them in the saddlebags then carried them upstairs and shoved it all under the bed.

Not wanting to see anyone for the rest of the day, Cathy laid down on the bed spread and tried to sleep.

At supper time a light knock sounded at the door.

"Cathy, Dear, are you alright?" Clara said through the door.

"Yes. I just took a slight headache from the sun today. It's nothing. I'll be fine tomorrow morning."

"I knew all that riding was not good for you. It is too strenuous for a young girl. We are going to have to find some indoor activities to occupy you." "Yes, ma'am," Cathy said.

"Sleep well, Child," Clara called to her.

"Thank you. Good night," Cathy replied.

Clara's footsteps faded away.

Cathy stared wide eyed at the ceiling. All she had to do now was wait until the house became quiet.

The hallway clock chime echoed through the quiet house. Cathy forced her eyes open then realizing she had fallen asleep, she crawled out of bed. The world felt heavy on her shoulders as she forced herself to hurry. Time was her worst enemy now.

She dressed quickly in black riding skirt, boots and dark blue blouse and pinned her hair securely in a hasty bunch on top of her head. That accomplished, she got down on her hands and knees and pulled the full pillow case she had prepared earlier from under the bed. My gun, she thought and retrieved the small pistol Ray had given her from under the mattress. She secured the gun in her waist band, flung the full pillowcase over her shoulder. One last look around the room, she dimmed the lamps and tip toed to the back stairs.

Fortunately, the steps were kept dimly lit during the night. Cathy stepped as lightly as she could with the heavy load, thankful for not having to walk down in the dark. At the bottom she hesitated for a moment to be sure no one still wandered about then she skittered out the door toward the stable.

The three-quarter moon set a pale glow to the trees and ground alike providing just enough light for Cathy to make her way. But once inside, total darkness engulfed her and she had to rely completely on her sense of touch to get around. She found Fancy in her usual stall near the door and saddled her quickly. She would have to go deeper inside to find a horse for Ray.

151

The stable grew darker as she walked deeper inside. The scratching of tiny claws sent chills of fear up the back of her neck but she continued to walk, hands extended straight in front of her, until she bumped into a warm furry wall.

Buck started and stepped back away from her stomping his big hooves noisily on the dirt floor.

"Buck! You're here. Oh, thank God," Cathy whispered in delight. "Come on, Boy, don't be afraid." She patted him along his side and neck feeling his big muscles relax under her hands.

A modicum of vision returned as her eyes grew accustomed to the dark. She half looked; half felt her way around the stall. She found Ray's saddle across a stool and sliding it close to Buck she lifted the saddle as high as she could but could not lift it high enough. She stood on the stool and lifted again this time with a pushing motion. The straps swung free giving her momentum she needed. In one last hard push she threw out away from herself in the direction of Buck's back. It landed with a loud whop.

Buck snorted in protest but Cathy didn't stop to apologize. She jumped down and fastened the cinches securely then slipped on the bridle and led him up beside Fancy. She hoisted the saddlebags and filled pillowcase and tied them securely to Buck's saddle horn then swung herself up on Fancy's back.

They started out slowly trying to move as quietly as possible but when Cathy found the town road and finally lost sight of the house, she urged the horses into a steady gallop.

Only a few buildings stood alight when Cathy arrived at the edge of town. This time she rode around behind the row of buildings and pulled up in back of the sheriff's office tying the horses against the building where the darkness would conceal them from passersby.

Stray hairs had begun to fall out of her hastily made nest and she ran her hands up over her hair to smooth it back into place. She straightened her clothes and not giving herself time to change her mind she walked boldly into the sheriff's office without knocking.

Just like earlier, the office was empty. She had no more time to waste. Someone could come in at any minute. She rushed over to the sheriff's desk. No keys. She looked around the room and spotted a ring of large keys hanging on a nail by the bolted door that led to the cells. She grabbed them off the wall, lifted the bolt across the door to the cell doors and hurried in. Ray still laid on the floor unconscious. She unlocked the door and dropped down beside him. The ropes were tied tightly but she continued to pick at them until they finally came loose. Ray moaned as the blood rushed painfully into his numbed hands.

"He's alive," Cathy thought thankfully.

"Ray, Ray, it's me, Cathy. I've come to get you. We must leave. Now. Come on. Can you stand?"

He made no effort to move.

"You must help me. I can't carry you." She got to her feet and pulled at his arms.

He began to respond very weakly but through pure determination she managed to stand him up. Her breathing came deep and heavy as she labored against his full weight and using all her strength she partially pushed and partially dragged him out into the office. She rested a second then continued until they reached the back door.

Cathy looked out as best she could. No one was within her sight so she maneuvered him over to the horses.

Buck snorted and shook his head at the sight of Ray.

"Steady boy," she cooed to Buck as she propped Ray up against the big buckskin. "Ray," she said in his ear. "We've got to get you on this horse. Help me."

Ray tried to move his arms. Cathy helped him encircle the saddle horn. He pulled as hard as he could. Cathy pushed from behind and managed to get him across the saddle, stomach down.

"He's not going to stay up there," Cathy thought and ran back inside the office. She hadn't noticed before but several looped sections of rope hung on the wall. She grabbed the closest one as well as a gun and holster and ran outside. She hooked the gun belt

154

on her saddle horn, tied Ray as tightly as she could and jumped into her own saddle and they were off.

Not wanting to hurt Ray any more than necessary Cathy kept up a slow steady pace. She tried to stay away from the rougher areas although she found that difficult in the dark. She was weary from her earlier physical exertions and even though she had a nap, she longed for a nice soft bed to curl up in.

They rode for what seemed to Cathy to be hours. The moon had risen high in the sky giving more light to the surrounding land. Cathy looked out for as far as she could see and a funny thought occurred to her.

All the land looked the same, as if they were traveling in circles. Then she sat up straight in her saddle.

For all she knew they could be traveling in circles. She had no idea in what direction they were traveling or what direction they should take. She would have to be more alert, she thought, look for definite landmarks.

A crooked Tree stood off in the distance and Cathy studied it closely. The trunk was thick with age and one gnarled branch grew downward almost to the ground. From where Cathy sat in the dark it looked like a giant old man, steadying himself with a cane, standing alone in a battle against time and losing. She watched the tree as they plodded along and it disappeared from her sight. "Now, I'll watch for that tree, she thought, if I see it again, we are traveling in circles."

More hours passed and Cathy's eyelids became heavier and harder to hold open. Her weariness turned to soreness, then outright aching. She knew Ray couldn't take much more traveling. She had to find a place to stop. A terrible thought occurred to her. In the whole time since they had left the sheriff's office, Ray had not made one sound.

Stopping abruptly, she slid down off Fancy and stepped over to the Buckskin. She could not see Ray clearly in the darkness but she felt his back. Still breathing, ragged and uneven, but breathing. She remounted and prodded the horses on, feeling better for the short chance to stretch her legs.

The moon moved lower and the sky began to fade to a dark blue. In the faint light Cathy noted the land. The Rocky hills appeared flatter with less foliage. They were going somewhere, she thought, possibly north east. Then a thought struck her she had not considered before. She was in a new strange land with no knowledge of the dangers lurking around her. If Ray didn't survive then she probably wouldn't either. Lost in this vast wilderness with little food, she would surely parish. As these forlorn thoughts raced across her exhausted mind Cathy looked out over the wide plain. Dawn broke through in a burst of pink and yellow. She blinked her tired eyes against the bright light. A distant object caught her attention. It looked like a square wooden structure like a cabin or a house. She hurried the horses on, afraid if she didn't, it, like the night sky, would disappear.

Chapter XIV

Cathy kicked open the weather warped door and grimaced at the filthy sight beyond. What she had thought to be a house or a cabin in the distance turned out to be a dilapidated shack. Dirt stood an inch thick over the bare wooden floor and it was obvious to Cathy nothing but spiders and mice had lived here for several years. There was no furniture, just one room and a fireplace at one end with a huge black iron pot hanging in the hearth. But Cathy told herself, there was a well outside and the shack was still a shelter.

The sun burned a brilliant gold as it peeked when she ran back out to the horses grazing happily just outside the door. She would rub them down later, she thought, taking the full pillowcase and saddlebags down from Buck's saddle and hurried back into the house. She emptied the contents of the pillowcase and using it as a dust mop she cleaned off an area of the floor and spread out one of the clean white linen sheets. Then taking Buck's reins she led him in

157

through the door as close to the sheet as she could. She untied Ray's hands holding him tight around the waist. Ray slid slowly down Buck's side. When his feet touched the floor, Cathy held fast to his body trying to guide him into a controlled fall protecting his head from impact. He hit the floor and groaned in protest.

"Sorry," she said centering him on the sheet.

Buck's big hooves clomped nervously on the wooden floor. Taking him by the bit she led him back outside, unsaddled both horses and tethered them where they could graze easily on the overgrown brush around the shack.

Cathy stopped for a moment to catch her breath. She had much to do and little time in which to do it. Surprisingly, she felt confident in her nursing skills. She knew what she needed to do, all she had to do was stay focused. She went straight to work.

It took nine trips to the well to fill the iron pot with water using the old wooden bucket she found outside then four more to gather twigs and dried grass to build a fire. With a sulfur from Ray's saddlebag, she lit the fire and swung the old iron pot over the fire to heat the water. She turned back to Ray.

The first step, she thought, was to find out how badly he was hurt. The sharp hunting knife she took from his saddle bags cut easily through what was left of his clothes but some areas of the wounds had dried sealing pieces of his shirt within them. Carefully, she removed every piece she could with the knife then she used the bucket to dip out some of the boiling water from the iron pot. Taking the other sheet from the pillowcase, she made strips of the clean cloth, dipped them in the boiled water, and held them against the stuck places until they came free.

Ray moaned in protest but she continued working until he lay naked before her. Once able to inspect him thoroughly, he did not seem to be in as bad a shape as she had expected. His body was covered with surface cuts, welts and burns but no bones appeared to be broken. If she could stave off infection, he could be ready to ride in as little as a week. But she would have to be diligent in his care.

Cathy bathed him with the boiled water and applied the antiseptic she had brought from the ranch on every wound. He fought her weakly but she managed to get it done. The antiseptic ointment felt thick and gooey on her hands so she used this as moisture to massage his chest, arms and back then covered him with the other clean sheet.

This done, she turned her attention to food. Ray needed nourishment to heal and she knew he hadn't had food in at least two days. She took the dried beans and bacon from the pillowcase. After washing an old log, she found beside the fireplace, she cut half of the bacon into large chunks then dumped the beans and bacon pieces into the boiling water over the fire. They tumbled over each other as the roiling water boiled in the big pot. Cathy watched them longingly, wishing they were ready to eat right now. She watched until her legs began to feel slightly shaky and a nagging cramp grew between her shoulder blades.

"I had better see to the horses and gather more firewood," she thought lying back on the floor. "I'll rest a minute then go out and have a look around." She closed her eyes and drifted off into a sound sleep.

"No, don't," the words screamed in her head but try as she might she could not make them come through her mouth. She tried to run but her arms and legs were jelly wriggling grotesquely every time she gave them a command. And still he came. Walking toward her, his one toothed grin etched across his face, his beady eyes bulging out at her like a malformed gargoyle leering at his helpless prey. He came closer and blood began to flow like a waterfall from behind his ears down his arms and off the tips of his outstretched fingers. She tried to pull away but her body wouldn't move and her screams grew into aching knots inside her silent throat. He reached out and at the touch of his icy fingers, Cathy's eyes flew open and she sat bolt upright becoming instantly awake.

A dream, she thought, and for a minute she felt lost staring dazedly at the inside of the dirty old cabin. It had grown dark except for a few coals glowing in the fireplace and a slight chill had crept in around her. Ray tossed restlessly. The covers had become wrapped around his waist and neck. Cathy scooted over to him and he began to mutter softly through his dry lips. She unwound the sheets and spread them back out. In the faint light she could see a flush over his tanned skin. His forehead and stomach felt warm to her fingers. The wounds looked clean, no festering or odor, but some of the skin around them appeared to Cathy to be swelling and turning an angry red. Worried, she bathed him in cold water and reapplied the antiseptic. A cold rag on his forehead calmed him some, and he licked thirstily at the drops of water she dribbled on his mouth.

A low grumbling erupted from Cathy's stomach.

"I have to eat right now," she thought and leaving Ray for a minute she crossed over to the fireplace and oblivious to manners or appearances she scooped up a handful of soupy beans and ate until her stomach felt relaxed and heavy. She washed her face and hands in the remainder of the water then fetched a fresh bucketful.

This accomplished, she settled in at Ray's side. Cathy knew the night would grow long. Fever was a persistent enemy. But, she thought, so was she. Taking the first wet rag from the bucket of cool water, she mopped over his entire body. She waited an estimated thirty minutes, then repeated the treatment. She continued throughout the night. At first, he fought trying to fend her off but as her

161

soothing voice and gentle touch seemed to calm him, he finally settled into a calm sleep.

Around day break Cathy felt Ray's chest and forehead. The fever had broken a few hours earlier but she continued bathing him until she felt sure the fever would not return. She got to her feet slowly to give the ache in her back time to subside then went out to check on the horses and gather more fuel for the fire. The horses drank the water she brought them, they seemed to be happy eating the wild grasses within their reach. They had cleared the area around them so she moved them down a short distance where a fresh crop of green plants grew. The two horses set straight to work on the new meal.

"They look rested and content," she thought and turned to her next chore.

Endless numbers of sticks and dried grass littered the front of the cabin. Cathy gathered extra for later use and returned to her patient inside.

The fireplace flared instantly when she added new fuel. She stirred the beans in the big iron pot and positioned them back over the fire to reheat. Ray's wounds looked much better this morning, she thought, but she applied the remainder of the salve and looked at the empty jar.

"Perfect," she thought. Using it as a cup, she dipped some of the warmed bean juice from the pot. Carefully she lifted Ray's head and sat down cuddling him comfortably in her lap.

162

"Here is some nice soup. Open up," she said softly into his ear.

To her surprise his lips parted. She lifted his head and managed to pour some of the warm nourishment down his throat.

"Easy, easy," she cooed as he struggled to get the liquid down. He took two more swallows then she placed his head carefully into her lap. She stroked his brow until his breathing grew regular in sleep. Cathy closed her eyes and let her head fall forward. Ray mumbled something and nestled closer into her soft belly and slept peacefully.

Around noon, Cathy moved Ray's head from her lap and placed it gently on the floor. Her arms and legs felt sore and reluctant to move as she worked, stoking the fire and rinsing out the improvised mug. Washing herself helped to relieve the stiffness. She removed the pins from her hair, ran her fingers through to remove as many tangles as she could, then plaited it into one long braid that hung down the middle of her back. Returning to Ray, she sat down beside him on the sheet. His breathing sounded loud and even in the silent room. Cathy felt relieved. He was better, she thought, and reached out to smooth the tousled black hair that hung down over his forehead. He moved closer at her touch, like a child needing comfort and her heart went out to him. A wave of tenderness came over her and suddenly the only thing that mattered to her was to have Ray well. She kissed his cheek.

An unusual craving for boiled eggs and kidneys came over her and glancing around the room she spotted the pot of stale beans hanging on the swing arm in the fireplace. Her empty stomach contracted in rebellion and she lifted her fist in the air.

"As God is my witness," she swore out loud, "if I live through this, I will never look another bean in the eye again."

Cathy heard a faint laugh and looked down to see Ray clutching his chest, his face a distorted grimace of pain. Cathy jumped up and grabbed the empty salve jar, dipped it full of water and lifted his head to drink. He took two good sips then began to relax. Cathy placed him back into her lap and gently stroked his forehead.

"Your fever has broken," she said gratefully.

He looked up at her in confusion.

"Fever? What fever? Where are we?" he said as if just noticing the unfamiliar cabin.

"I'm not sure," Cathy said. "We rode northeast for about twelve hours at a very slow pace."

"Twelve hours from where?" he said.

Cathy's eyes widened. What if he didn't remember? What if he wasn't able to find his way to where ever they were supposed to be going?

"Don't you remember? You were curled up on the floor of the sheriff's office tied hand and foot. I came in and helped you out."

He stared at her for another minute then memories started coming back. He was in jail. A leather strap made a splashing sound as it tore at his back, a poker glowing vibrant orange in the fire and his flesh, his own flesh, burning into an acrid foul smoke. He remembered the sheriff smiling the entire time.

He looked up at the ceiling.

"Oh yeah, the jail," he mumbled.

Relief flooded over Cathy.

Ray looked around the cabin.

"You say you have some beans?"

Cathy filled the jar from the big pot and brought it back to him.

"Drag my saddle over here," he said.

Cathy pulled it up by his head. He raised up slowly and she pushed it under his back careful to lift the sheet over it still conscious of the danger of infection. He leaned back into a half sitting position and took the beans Cathy held out.

"I have no spoons," she apologized.

He smiled and that old amusement played about his lips.

"I can manage," he said scooping the beans out with two fingers and handing the jar back to her. "You say you helped me out of jail. How?"

She looked away from him uncertain whether or not to tell him the whole story.

It wasn't easy," she hedged.

A thought occurred to Ray as Cathy spoke. Weston's men were probably out looking for him right now. If they found them, he would probably be killed right away but Cathy wouldn't be that lucky.

"How long have we been here?" he asked

"Two days and two nights," she answered.

"We have to leave as soon as possible."

Cathy looked at him in surprise. She wanted to argue with him. He wasn't healed enough to travel. But he was right. They had been stationary too long. And besides, if she gave him any trouble, he might just decide to leave her here alone to fend for herself.

"When?" she said.

He considered her for a minute.

"I'll rest today, we'll leave tonight." His tone softened. "I'm afraid you'll have to do most of the work."

She smiled and walked over to sit down beside him.

"Lay back and let me see how your wounds are this morning."

He obeyed without another word and sat still as she turned him from side to side, front to back, examining his raw skin, gently touching here and there. The swelling had gone and the redness seemed some better. The bruises were turning darker as bruises did before fading away. Overall, he seemed much improved.

Absorbed in her evaluations Cathy hadn't noticed Ray was watching her. He clasped his hands behind his head enjoying the feel of those gentle fingers running over him intimately. She leaned over to get a closer look at a burn on his chest and the shirt fell away from her body allowing a perfect view of a lovely pear-shaped breast. It looked ripe for the suckling and the idea loomed vivid in his mind when Cathy looked up into his face. His velvety brown eyes bore down on her and she could feel the force of his desire through every nerve in her body.

Suddenly self-conscious, she clutched the opened shirt to her throat and slowly rose and went over to tend the fireplace.

Disappointed to see her go, he leaned back against the saddle letting heavy lids drop over his eyes and a slow private smile spread across his soft sensuous lips.

Actually, Cathy had little to do to get herself ready to leave. She emptied the large pot and wiped it out leaving it clean for the next occupants, cleaned out the fireplace and watered and fed the horses. Ray slept on and off all day. She took advantage of one of these naps to wash and change back into her clothes. As night drew near, she took the bottle of whiskey she had taken from the library and handed it to Ray. "I thought this might ease the pain some."

"Thanks," he said taking it from her.

She waited until he had taken a few sips before kneeling down beside him.

"I'm going to tear this sheet now and bandage you up before I help you dress."

"Alright," he said. "Help me sit up."

After helping Ray dress and saddling the horses, Cathy was glad to see how much easier it was to get Ray on his horse this time. Although he still needed help, he was conscious and able to help some. They traveled slowly at first stopping to rest every few hours.

For the first two days, finding food was a problem. Cathy wished over and over she hadn't been so quick to throw away the stale beans and bacon. Eating rotten beans was better than starving to death, she thought. But even on a diet of wild berries and water, Ray became stronger as time went by.

On the afternoon of the third day they stopped beside a cool creek. The water felt like heaven as Cathy splashed it on her face and let it dribble down her arms. She had just finished washing when two shots exploded not too far from where she stood. She jumped nearly off the ground and it took every ounce of balance she had to keep from falling headlong into the stream. Regaining her footing she turned immediately to look for Ray but he was nowhere to be seen. Her heart pumped faster and faster as she waded out into the creek to grab the horse's reins and pull them forcibly from the water into a brushy area nearby. In her hunger weakened state she found it hard to remain calm. The trees seemed to sway around her even though no wind blew. The image of Ray lying out there somewhere shot and dying tortured her mind. She heard footsteps crackling through the sun dried under brush, her breath stopped dead in her throat.

If they had caught Ray, she must get to Oklahoma by herself, she thought frantically. Just then Buck lifted his nose into the air and whinnied softly. Ray stepped out into the clearing, two small furry creatures dangling from his hand.

"Food," she said and hurried out of her hiding place. The two horses followed along behind her.

"We eat tonight," Ray said smiling proudly. "Do you know how to clean a rabbit?"

Cathy eyed the limp creatures longingly.

"No, but I can learn or if I can't, I'll just eat them hair and all."

Ray laughed.

169

"You have to have a strong stomach," he warned her. "There is only one knife so I'll do the first one and you can do the other."

"All right," she agreed and followed him eagerly her mouthwatering in anticipation of a good meal.

Ray watched in disbelief when shortly after he started, Cathy took the knife from him and shooed him away to start the fire. Her fingers worked with the skill of a trapper. But after all, Cathy thought, cleaning a rabbit was not much different from cleaning a chicken. She had done that many times. In the market, whole chickens were far cheaper than already trussed ones. She had practically become an expert at detecting which birds hid the most meat under their dense feather coats. She skewered the two scrawny carcasses onto a sturdy-looking stick and turned them over to Ray. They took less time to cook than Cathy expected and even less time to eat. She didn't want to fall asleep so she sat by the fire and closed her eyes enjoying the feel of warm food in her stomach.

Ray sat back against a rustling cottonwood tree and watched the firelight dance across Cathy's blouse jumping in and out of the tempting hollow at the base of her neck.

"Cathy by firelight," he thought and for a second, he longed to make a bed of soft grass to lie her in and make love to her all night. But now was not the time. He had to find Bessie Camden. But he didn't want to lose Cathy in the process.

"We better get moving," he said to Cathy.

"I'll get the horses," she said.

"I'll tend to the fire then saddle 'em," he said. "We've got some hard miles coming up." Cathy smiled and went to gather the horses.

"Let's go find Bessie," she said.

Chapter XV

Cathy felt herself falling from Fancy's back into a pair of warm strong arms. She slipped her hands around Ray's neck and cuddled closer resting her cheek against his chest. Ray carried her into the white limestone house through the parlor into the bedroom and laid her in the middle of the soft feather bed. She opened her eyes to see Ray lighting a lamp that stood on a small table nearby.

"Where are we?" she asked. Her voice sounded groggy and slurred in her ears.

"On my ranch in Oklahoma." Ray said.

"Oh," she replied not having the faintest idea where Oklahoma was. Her eyes fell shut again. She teetered on the edge of wakefulness and sleep feeling her last ounce of strength drain away.

"Am I dreaming?" she asked.

"I don't know," Ray said.

"Remember the night when you told me that if I wanted to know the part of the night I was drugged and can't remember just come to you and you wouldn't turn me down?"

"Yes, very clearly," he said softly.

"Will you please show me now?"

"Yes, Ma'am," he whispered.

Ray took off his clothes and left them on the floor. The bed sagged as he climbed in next to her. She reached out to him and he pulled her into his arms. She felt his lips warm and gentle teasing her with his tongue until she began to respond in kind. He kissed her deeply, holding her tightly, then taking his hands from around her, began teasing her lips again. She felt her body start to move against him wanting more. In response, his hands started to move over her, caressing, soothing. He began to massage her toes, then her feet, then her calves and thighs. He caressed her all over. She couldn't still her body. The more he touched her the more she wanted his touch. Then he parted her legs. Her first reflex was to press them together again, but he nudged them apart again and began kissing her in her most intimate places. His lips and tongue teased her, taunted her, made her moan, reaching for something unknown. Just as she felt her body growing closer to what she craved, he stopped and began kissing her deeply on the lips again. Disappointed, she moaned in need and Ray responded and filled her with his manhood. Making slow easy movements, he took his time, massaging her nipples, her most intimate places, then began moving inside her increasing his movement until in a burst of excruciating pleasure explained every longing, satisfied every need she could imagine leaving her limp and fulfilled. Ray held her close as his pleasure subsided kissing her deep and whispering words she could not understand. She kissed him back whispering words that only her heart could understand then drifted into a wonderful happy quiet sleep.

Cathy shivered and curled up into a smaller ball trying to ward off the cold that seemed determined to wake her. But it did no good. An icy draft crept up her bare buttocks through a tiny opening between her thighs and whistled up her belly like a blue norther in December. She reached out, beating the bed beside her feeling for the cover. Reluctantly, she opened her eyes to search in earnest. The white walls glared out at her in the bright morning sunlight. Momentarily confused, she looked around the unfamiliar room.

Where was she, she thought, when her gaze settled on a strange statue standing in the corner. Then the statue moved and Cathy realized the statue was alive.

"Who are you?" she demanded very impolitely then remembered this was most likely the woman's home she, of course being the guest.

"I'm sorry. That sounded terribly rude of me. How do you do?" Cathy corrected holding her legs together and trying to cover her bare breasts with her hands.

The woman was short, barely five feet, Cathy thought, and exceptionally wide for her height. Her black hair hung in two tight braids to her thick waist. Her strong forehead jutted out over a wide flat nose and thick lips. Her black eyes watched Cathy closely, like the eyes in a portrait she had seen once, following her everywhere and never moving. The woman could have been a character in one of her nightmares, Cathy thought.

"I'm Catherine Wilmershire. And you are...?" she tried again.

The woman did not speak. Instead, she plunged her fist into her huge bosom and pulled out a folded piece of paper. She held it out to Cathy never letting her gaze waiver.

Cathy eyed her nervously then leaned enough forward to snatch the paper away with her fingertips. She sat back and read the note quickly.

Cathy,

Had to go. Urgent business. Decide what to do
with you when I get back. Yellow Cloud will take care
of you.

Ray

"Please God, let him find Bessie," she said holding
the note against her heart.

Seeing her distress, Yellow Cloud waddled around
the bed and picked up the gray blanket from where it
had been kicked onto the floor. She wrapped it
snugly around Cathy's shaking body and hugged her
like she would have any frightened lost child.

For the first few days, Yellow Cloud restricted
Cathy to the bed, waiting on her new charge hand
and foot. She brought warm baths and piping meals
into the little room. She had even managed to find
some old clothes, out dated and slightly too large, but
serviceable. When Cathy was finally allowed to get
up, she spent her days with Yellow Cloud cleaning
and cooking in the tiny limestone house.
Occasionally, the thick walls would start to move in
on Cathy. Afraid of going too far away, she took
short walks. She had met Joe, Yellow Cloud's
husband, on one of these. He too was stone faced
and quiet. He spoke English but very seldom did
preferring to be left alone to work. But, through
perseverance, Cathy managed to pester a few facts
out of him.

She found out that Joe and Yellow Cloud were
members of the Kiowa Indian tribe that had migrated

to this territory from their home on the great plains
of central Texas. When the daughter of the chief had
married the white man, Mr. Michaels, the chief sent
the couple along to care for her and after she died in
childbirth, Mr. Michaels had asked them to stay and
help raise his boy. They agreed. For their loyalty to
his wife, Mr. Michaels gave them the gift of the
house, two horses and a place of honor in his
household.

Yellow Cloud never spoke English. Feeling this
would be disloyal to all the ancestors who had died at
the hands of the white man, she only communicated
by Kiowa sign language. At first Cathy had found
that awkward but as time passed, she learned to read
the woman's gestures with ease. Yellow Cloud
understood every word Cathy said to her, Cathy
suspected, and she was probably quite fluent in
English but she admired the woman's loyalty to her
beliefs and the honor she paid to those she loved.

Cathy also learned from Joe that he visited a town
close by to purchase food and supplies. Ray had left
money with him for anything she needed.

"That was considerate of him" she thought. But
she couldn't take it. If there was a town there was
probably employment. By the time Ray returned to
do something with her as he said in his note, she
could be living a comfortable life without his help.

Long lazy days melted into cool quiet nights but
for all of her resting Cathy seemed to grow more
listless by the day needing a nap every afternoon.

Oddly, her appetite was better than usual so she was not ill. She was simply letting herself grow lazy, she thought. A long walk and a trip into town would do her a world of good. She found Joe and asked if she could ride into town with him tomorrow. But the next morning she felt so dizzy and nauseated she barely made the walk across the room to grab the wash basin before spewing vomit everywhere.

Yellow Cloud appeared by her side and using a wet cloth cleaned her face and helped her back to the bed. Cathy looked up at Yellow Cloud and when made to move away Cathy threw her arms around her shoulders and refused to let go. Yellow Cloud patted Cathy gently on her back. She could see the fear and confusion on her face. She sat Cathy on the bed and stepped away. Reaching out, she placed one hand on her belly and crooking the elbow of her other arm she rocked it back and forth as if rocking a baby.

Cathy stared at her for a moment then covering her face with both hands, she flung herself face down into her pillow.

Ray brought Buck to a stop in front of the white two-story house and climbed the front steps three at a time.

"Father," he called as he crossed the entry hall and strode toward the oak paneled study. Before he could even grab the brass door knobs, the double doors opened. His father stood there smiling in surprise and relief.

Bill Michaels pulled his son into a strong embrace and led him into the study. He poured them both a double brandy, handed one to Ray then sat down in his leather chair behind his desk. Ray took one of the smaller chairs in front of the desk and drew a long sip from his glass.

"Well, what did you find out?" his father said.

All the way from the little house he had been wondering how to tell his father the news. Now that he was here, he decided to tell him straight out. He looked down at the floor and shook his head.

"It' not good, Dad."

His father braced himself for bad news.

"Did you see Bessie? Is she—dead?"

"Yes, I saw her. She was alive, then. I'm not so sure about now." Ray tossed down the rest of his drink and told his father the whole story omitting the part about Cathy.

His father listened without speaking except to swear under his breath now and then.

So, what do you think we should do now? He asked when Ray finished.

"We need to hurry if we are going to try to save her. We need to notify Senator Camden, pick a few men that can be trusted and get to London as fast as possible. We need to keep all this quiet. If the people who have her are spooked in any way, Bessie could disappear forever."

Bill Michaels stared at Ray for a minute.

"All right, Son. I'm with you. I'll wire Senator Camden. We'll work everything out. I'll try to have a working plan set for departure tomorrow before sun up. You go get some rest. I'll have food sent up to your room."

Up in his room, Ray let the hot water soak his exhausted muscles until they began to relax only moving when a tender spot from one of the healing wounds scraped against the side of the tub. He thought about Cathy and how she had cared for him. Soft hands, he thought. She had looked like a ginger haired squaw in his buckskin shirt with her hair braided down her back and her long shapely legs and feet bare. If he could see her just once more before he left, he thought, but he knew there was no time. When he returned, he thought, he would have time to explore those delicious thighs and listen to her sigh softly in his ear as desire engulfed them both and carried them to contentment again.

Chapter XVI

Cathy walked up St. Gerrard in London carrying the small brocade satchel she had bought in New York. Several weeks had passed since she had ridden into town with Joe back in America. Fortunately, she had found a dressmaker who worked out of her house. Cathy had bought several home spun dresses the seamstress had sown to use as samples. The seamstress seemed thrilled to have a customer willing to purchase all three plus a petticoat and a hairbrush. Cathy wore the bright red oversized wool dress Yellow Cloud had given her. The ramshackle wardrobe at best made her look dowdy and odd. But it got her home without incident and that was good, she thought.

This trip had been easier than the first. After visiting the dressmaker, she found the stagecoach office and purchased a ticket to Kansas City where she caught the train to New York. From New York she had enough of the money Ray had left for her to book passage to London.

Now she stood at those familiar front steps and looked up at what had once been the boundaries of her world. It used to seem so plain and indifferent as if merely tolerating her existence within its walls hardly noticing her coming and going. But today its closed and curtained windows seemed to leer down at her, a jeering mocking smirk across its stony façade as if to say she would never escape from here again. Had she the strength, she would have sat down just where she was in the middle of the walk and cried. But her back ached unmercifully and her feet felt swollen from the long walk from the docks. She had been nauseous every morning on land and sea. She simply had no more energy left for a good cry. Besides, she had to think about what she would say to Leonard.

"What does it matter," she thought. "I have the greatest gift God can give, a beautiful baby, a piece of Ray, to love and care for."

A warm afternoon breeze like the caress of a tender touch blew across her face and she sighed. If only he had wanted her, she would have stayed. But he made himself clear in his note.

"I'll decide what to do with you when I get back," he had said.

"Decide what to do with me, indeed," she said aloud. "I decide what to do with me. I'm not some reticent frightened calf in need of branding."

She looked up at the house. She felt too tired to think about it anymore. She just wanted to go up to her old room and lay down on her old cot.

She climbed the steps slowly and opened the door. Setting her bag on the first step of the stairway and looked around the old familiar house in astonishment.
Not much had changed in her three-month absence. She had expected to see the place in a complete tangle, but everything looked neat and well looked after.

A haughty voice came from behind her.

"Hello, Dear Sister." Leonard walked up behind her with a note of surprise in his voice.

His brows raised in question but Cathy remained silent. Instead, she perused his handsome rather expensively tailored suit and raised her eyebrow in kind.

"How have you been, Dear Brother?" she said holding her head up and adding a touch of haughtiness to her own voice.

Cathy looked the entryway up and down. The only noise in the house was the ticking of the old clock on the parlor mantle.

"The house looks wonderful. You have done a good job of keeping it up."

"Me," Leonard laughed. "Dear Girl, unlike you, I have never cleaned a house in my life. I have engaged two new maids in your absence."

Leonard had always enjoyed baiting her into angry responses, then laughing at her for being a hysterical female.

"But that was then and this is now," she thought giving him a cool smile.

Leonard's smile dropped slightly.

"Let's sit in the parlor." He led her in then sat himself in their father's favorite leather chair. She sat in one of the wooden side chairs and arranged the heavy red dress as if it was an expensive travel ensemble. "Catherine, you must understand something. I am the head of the house now and I will not be questioned, about finances or any of it." He tipped his head up higher and looked down his nose at her.

He was still trying to set her off, she realized. She held her smile steady.

"I'm not letting him win this time," she thought.

"Yes, Leonard," she said calmly placing her hands in her lap.

Just then, the front door slammed and Cathy looked around to see Peter Weston striding across the front hall and into the parlor. He saw Cathy and stopped, speechless at first. He and Leonard exchanged unreadable glances then hurried toward

Cathy taking both of her hands in his and kissing each one.

Cathy flushed and fought to not pull her hands away. He spoke to her but the only words in her head were the last words she heard him utter, the cool unfeeling pronouncement of Ray's death.

"Catherine," Leonard interrupted their greetings, "The maid is off for a few week's holiday, will you be so kind as to take her place and prepare us some nice tea then we can all have a nice chat."

"Of course," she said thankful for the chance to leave the room.

The kitchen was in good order also, she thought, her hands busy filling the copper kettle that always sat out on the stove, taking the tea tray from the top shelf of the pantry, ordinary activities almost completed themselves they were so ingrained from years of habit.

"What am I going to do?" she kept thinking until a wave of nausea set the room spinning. "Not that," she thought bracing herself on the counter and forcing herself to relax. She was not going to give in now, she thought. Straightening her back to full height, she dabbed cool water over her eyes, pinched her cheeks, then carried the tea service into the parlor.

"How nice," Peter said taking the heavy tray out of her hands and placing it on the small table in front

185

of the loveseat. Common sense told her not to sit too close to him but not wanting to appear afraid she seated herself directly beside him and served the tea. Leonard had left in her absence leaving her alone with Peter. He seemed to be conflicted about something while she smiled back trying not to look nervous. Finally, he put the cup down. "Very good tea. Your mother took her new maid with her to Bath, Peter said, "and we haven't had a decent refreshment since I arrived." His voice sounded friendly and polite but his gaze wandered over her body as he talked.

"I didn't know my mother had a new maid," Cathy said.

"There are a number of things you don't know, Catherine. And a few I don't know, too. For instance, where have you been and why did you run away like that?"

There it was, the question she didn't want to hear. She looked down at her lap picking helplessly at the rough fabric of her skirt.

"I-it was," she started and a quiver softened her voice. "I was afraid," she groped and forced herself to look up into his cold blue eyes.

Afraid of what?" he asked.

"Of you." She ran the tip of her tongue around the edge of her lips. That night of the party when you wanted to come to my bedroom. I didn't know what to do. You were so strong."

186

Peter laughed low and throaty and trailed his fingers lightly up and down her arm.

"I wasn't going to hurt you," he said.

Cathy shifted nervously.

"Where did you go, Cathy?" he asked more insistently.

"I rode into town, took the stage coach to Kansas City then rode the railroad to New York. There I boarded the Queen's Pride for home. "The story was so close to the truth it rolled very convincingly off her tongue.

"I see," Peter said. "What did you use for money?

Cathy looked him straight in his eyes. "I sold Fancy."

"You must have gotten a good price."

She looked at the worn rug beneath her scuffed boots.

"Yes, I did," she said.

He closed his hand around her upper arm and squeezed.

"Catherine, I don't know if you're lying or not." He said it so quietly she almost did not hear.

"I'm not lying!" she insisted.

"All right, Catherine, I believe you. You are such an empty-headed innocent I have to believe you." He sounded more bitter than teasing. "I am going to tell you the whole story but once I do, you are part of it. There will be no more running away."

Cathy looked surprised. She thought she had just gotten away from the intrigue on the Weston Ranch only to find out it had followed her home. She didn't want to be involved in their evil deeds. She had a baby to protect. Before she could object, Peter continued.

"Certain circumstances exist in America today that could possibly, or I might even say will probably lead that country into a civil war. I know that would be a terrible thing for the Yankees but sometimes where a war can mean hardship and destruction in the country where it occurs, it can mean a period of improvement and prosperity for other countries not directly involved. Increased trade, demand for munitions accelerate progress at a rate that could never be matched under normal conditions. Beef cattle will be worth their weight in gold."

Cathy listened intently hardly believing what he was saying.

"As it happens, there is a group of very rich and important men here in England who would like to see this war take place and we have devised several ways of, shall we say, shifting the wind in that direction. My father is a member of this group. Father, Leonard and I are involved in one of these maneuvers right now. You see, through some very simple actions we were able to apprehend the young daughter of a United States Senator and using his daughter's safety as leverage, we have his influence at our mercy."

Cathy couldn't help herself.

"How could you do such a thing to a child! What have you done with her?" she yelled.

"Catherine, don't be so emotional about this. The girl is fine. She is upstairs sleeping. I am taking care of her. Don't you see? This is good for your country. All Englishmen will benefit from this. Look at your brother. He is becoming quite wealthy. Your mother and sisters are well taken care of and you, lovely Catherine, I will take care of you, too."

His pale blue-eyed gaze swept over her and she shuddered at the pure evil it belied. As if in a trance, he pulled the pins from her hair and watched it spill all shining and soft down her chest. He stroked the curling tresses letting his fingers linger on the very tips of her nipples.

"Of course, you know marriage is out of the question," he said. "Not after the way you ran off. I don't know where you've been or who you have been with." A slow smile crept across Peter's mouth. "But I can care for you, set you up in a house of your own."

Then, before she could stop him, he pinioned her to the couch, his grinning face a frightening blur of pale blue eyes and pink tinted skin. Hard lips nipped at her earlobe and breathed a wintry path along her cheek to her mouth where they pressed painfully against her teeth.

"See," he whispered in her ear, "you're not such a cold little bitch," he said and to Cathy's relief, stood and adjusted his slimly cut trousers. "I know you're tired. Go upstairs to freshen up. Take a rest. Leonard and I have an appointment we must keep. But I'll be back—tonight," the pronouncement sounding to Cathy like a threat.

Leonard's footsteps thumped on the stairs as he stepped down to the hall and strode into the parlor carrying Peter's short cape and bowler hat.

"We'd best be off," he said transferring the cape to Peter's arm and handing him the hat.

"Did you tell her?"

"Yes," Peter answered taking the hat with the tips of his fingers then bouncing it as if gauging its weight.

Leonard turned to Cathy.

"Good. Now you understand and, like I said, I'll have no arguments out of you."

Cathy stood and faced him.

"Does Mother know about this?" she asked.

"Of course not. That's why I took such pains to send her and the girls away. And it's a damned nuisance having you here. It would have been so much more convenient if you had just stayed in America."

Cathy still refused to allow him to goad her into an argument.

The right corner of his mouth lifted contemptuously.

"Since you are here you may as well make yourself useful. That filthy little creature upstairs smells like a chamber pot. Scrub her and burn those awful clothes. Scrub down the room, too. That odor is fairly permeating the house. We may be taking her to the country tonight so have her ready."

He handed her a brass key.

"Yes, Leonard," she said hoping no one detected her excitement at being handed that key.

"Right," Leonard said. "We'll be back right on seven, have a supper ready."

The door clicked shut behind the two men. Cathy fell back onto the couch. How could any of this be true, she thought, staring at the key in her hand. War, kidnapping, she thought, then realizing whatever she was going to do, she would have to do it fast, she hurried up the stairs past the second floor to the small attic room that used to be her own. Taking the key from her hand, she slid it into the lock and turned the knob. The hinges creaked as she pushed the door open afraid of what she would find inside. A 'muted golden light from the late afternoon sun cast long shadows around the sparsely furnished room and set a strange yellow frame around the tiny skeletal girl who lay curled into a ball in the center of her coverless cot. Slowly, reluctantly, Cathy crept closer then stared down in horror. What had obviously been a beautiful young girl was now nothing more than a dry shell, her skin a sallow veil around her bones. Black circles ringed her lifeless eyes. And Leonard was right about the smell. She reeked of excrement.

Cathy's hand clamped over her mouth. She hurried over to the window and opened it wide. Fresh air rushed in around her. Giving the air a minute to clear, she glanced at the busy street below when a strange sight caught her eye. A man standing on the walk directly across the street was staring up at her. Seeing her take notice, the man quickly looked away. She wouldn't have thought twice about it except that he wore a long black winter cape and hat making him strangely out of place in the warm summer weather. She watched as he walked to the corner then she hurried back to the still form on the cot. She's dead, Cathy felt sure as she tugged gently at the grimy print dress the girl wore but with her clothes off, Cathy was relieved to see a slight rising and falling of the narrow rippling chest. Moving faster, Cathy grabbed the tin wash basin from under the cot, threw the dirty clothes in it and ran downstairs. The clothes were not worth the time to wash, Cathy realized, so she threw them out the back door. She filled the basin with cold water and hurried upstairs.

Back in the room, she scrubbed the girl using a rag she had brought from the kitchen. The water felt painfully cold on Cathy's hands and she kept expecting the girl to protest but during the entire bath she never once stirred. Worried, Cathy placed her hand in the center of the girl's chest and felt the faintest flutter of a heartbeat. They must have her drugged, she realized and Cathy had enough experience with nursing her father to know this girl was dangerously close to death. If she sleeps much longer, she will die, Cathy thought.

"I'm going to have to rouse her, give her strength to fight for her life."

Cathy ran down to Charlotte's room and stripped the clean linens from her bed and dug through her chest of drawers until she found an old night shirt that looked to be the right size. She hurried back upstairs and lifted the girl onto the floor long enough to make up the cot then she gently laid the girl back on it. She managed to pull the night shirt over her head and covered her protectively with the clean sheet. She placed her hand on the girl's chest again. Just the act of moving her around made her heart beat somewhat stronger. She needed more activity, Cathy thought, but before that, she needed food.

Unfortunately, the food pantries were empty except for a few slices of bread and some tea. Cathy started with weak tea laced with cream. She soaked the bread in the tea until it was squashy soft. Propping the frail child up on three freshly washed pillows, Cathy began coaxing small bites down the girl's throat. She began to choke, then began to swallow sucking at Cathy's fingers as she put in the bread. That should be enough for now she thought then taking one at a time, she lifted the girl's arms and legs bending each joint carefully as she had done for her paralyzed father only a few months before. This done, she rechecked her heartbeat and it seemed stronger to her touch. That's better, she thought sitting on the edge of the cot and brushing a honey brown curl off the girl's forehead.

How could anyone be this cruel to a child? Cathy wondered. Bessie, Ray called her. She was someone's daughter. How her parents must be suffering not knowing if she is dead or alive. Cathy's hand moved over her belly. Cathy stood, stretched, and crossed to the window. She started to close the shutters when she caught sight of the man in the black cloak staring up at her. She pulled the window shut.

"Closed for the night," she said to the mysterious stranger. "Go bother someone else."

She exercised Bessie's arms and legs again and had just started feeding her when the front door slammed. Leonard's voice echoed through the empty house.

"Catherine, come down here."

She hurried down the stairs smoothing her hair along the way. In her rush to care for Bessie, she had not taken the time to pin it back up. She straightened it the best she could and adjusted the crooked bodice of the loose-fitting dress.

"I am here," she said rushing into the parlor.

"I thought I told you to have dinner ready at seven," he said. "It is a quarter past. Why did you not cook supper?"

"Because there is no food in the house to cook," she said.

Out of reflex, Leonard's open palm drew back as if to strike her, then catching himself, he curled his fingers downward and dropped his hand to his side. Cathy didn't flinch or bat an eye. She glared at her brother with all the contempt she could muster.

"We shall dine out tonight. You will go to market tomorrow," he commanded.

"Suit yourself, Dear Brother," she said and walking to the door, held it open for the two men, closing and locking it behind them.

Up in her old room, Cathy thought through the two plans of escape she considered to get Bessie out of the house. Both seemed shaky at best, deadly if caught by Leonard or Peter. One plan involved escaping before the men returned from supper. One, she would carry Bessie to the hospital and beg for help and the other involved carrying her to the

195

Magistrate's office. Either one she would have to explain what has happened. Surely no would believe such a fantastical story even if it is the truth, she thought. But these were her choices and time was running out. If she waited much longer, the men would return, possibly take Bessie away never to be seen again.

Cathy looked out the window. The moon's pale glow illuminated the white sheet on the cot where Bessie slept. Only a light hovering of mist covered the seemingly deserted street. Her gaze swept to the corner but a sudden movement brought it back to the darkened buildings across the street. She looked deep into the shadows but saw nothing.

"It would be just like Leonard and Peter to be hiding out there waiting to see what she was going to do, she thought. She took her gun from the satchel she had brought from New York and dropped in the pocket of her dress.

Wrapping Bessie tightly in the sheet from the cot, she lifted her easily in her arms. The stairs seemed to creak a symphony as she slipped to the second floor. Not hearing any sounds, she hurried down to the first-floor hallway. The doorknob rattled awkwardly in her hand but she finally managed to turn it and they were suddenly outside, the damp air cold against her cheeks. In seconds she was down the stoop and running along the walkway, exhilaration carrying her on.

"We made it! she thought holding her bundle tighter against her chest when the unmistakable clop of footsteps sounded behind her.

"They must have seen me leave," she thought walking faster.

The footsteps sped up as well. They sounded closer. Panic set in and she began to run. Faster and faster, down St. Charles Street and around the corner onto Junespur Lane. House fronts passed by in a blur and still the footsteps followed gaining with every step. She ran on. The cool air burned her lungs as she sucked in big gulps, her heart pounded wildly against her chest, her bare feet began to bleed as the stones and refuse along the walkway cut away at her. She felt her legs tiring straining to reach forward, every muscle and tendon taut and aching. Her loose full skirt slapped against her ankles, too long without her boots. Keep going, she told herself feeling her pace slow then her foot caught the edge of the fabric. She felt the waistline rip as she tumbled forward. In one last effort she twisted catching the full weight of the falling girl upon her. Blue black sky spun over her and suddenly she was on her feet engulfed in black, strong arms holding her, a familiar heart beat against her ear. Then she was standing on her own again holding Bessie safely to her chest, being pulled forward by a warm firm hand, and the voice she had feared she would never hear again urged her on. "Come on, Cathy, you can make it," Ray said and they hurried away toward the docks.

Chapter XVII

Cathy plopped down onto the soft bunk and rubbed at her tired legs. Thinking back, she could not imagine how she had run all the way to the docks where the blonde man, Bessie's father, had been waiting for them.

It's hard to believe Leonard was mixed up with those evil people who would do that to an innocent girl, Cathy thought. Thank God Ray was able to track her down.

Cathy shook her head slowly. Maybe if I hadn't left home in such a rush, I could have overheard something or seen something sooner so Bessie wouldn't have had to suffer so. Even though she knew she hadn't had anything to do with Leonard's criminal activities, she still felt somewhat guilty for being related to him.

It had taken Ray nearly an hour to row down the river where the clipper ship Bessie's father owned bobbed easily in the ocean breezes. Once aboard, they wasted no time putting out to sea. She had followed Ray through the narrow passageway and watched as

he gently placed the sleeping girl in the large cabin at the end of the hall. Cathy had wanted to stay with her, but Ray had insisted she come into the smaller cabin to rest. Now the clipper creaked and tilted under her as its sails stretched out to catch the wind that would send them back to New Orleans.

There was a light tap on the door then a young man stepped into the room holding a bowl of water in one hand and a cup of hot black coffee in the other. He smiled shyly.

"Mr. Ray thought you might want to wash up. "

"Thank you," she said.

He set the items down on the small square table and backed out of the door.

The fresh water felt good as Cathy splashed it over her face letting stray drops run down her neck and into the high neckline of her red dress where it chafed the skin just below her throat. It felt good but the soles of her feet were on fire and the rough cotton wool dress worked against the crests of her sensitive breasts and at her waistline where the bodice and skirt met and bunched up around the tear. Not expecting to go out, she had not taken the time to put on her underclothes and the fabric of the homemade dress had taken its toll on her skin. Once she started, she could not stop. She took off the dress and rubbed the cold water all over with her bare hands then stripped a cool white sheet from the bunk and wrapped it around her. The sheet fit snuggly around her legs and hips so that she had to hobble instead of walk. She pulled it tightly around her chest and tucked the corner into the crease where her breasts mashed against each other threatening to pop out with every breath. Her copper hair hung loose and tangled to her waist. Her pale cheeks seemed to deepen the bluegreen hue in her eyes. With a little effort, she poured the remainder of the water into a circular puddle on the floor then sat down at the table sipping coffee and dabbling her burning feet.

Without warning the door opened. Ray ducked under the doorway and stepped into the room closing the door behind him. Cathy looked up, startled, then taken aback by his not knocking. His black mustache still grew thick and dangerous looking above his upper lip and his velvety brown eyes still swept over her leaving her as confused and breathless as before. Standing there with his tight black pants tucked into his black leather boots and his white lawn shirt opened down the front to where the soft patch of curly chest hair showed he looked like a warrior, brave and bold, returning from battle.

Each remained still, staring at the other for one time-suspended moment then Cathy looked away, down at the trembling coffee cup in her hand.

"I'm sorry. I didn't realize this was your room," she heard herself say and set the cup on the table before she sloshed coffee all over.

"How is the girl?" she asked trying to make her voice sound natural.

"Bessie is fine," he said and his low man's voice seemed to walk with feathered feet across her senses.

"She has to eat."

"Yes, she is being taken care of. She's with her father. He brought a doctor and a nurse with him."

His voice was very near her now. She jumped when he trailed his fingertips lightly across her shoulders.

"I'm afraid I have nothing to wear, she said feeling painfully self-conscious.

Ray chuckled softly and stepped closer pressing his firm warm legs against her back, letting his fingers play at the base of her wildly pulsating neck.

I owe you so much, Ray whispered so quietly Cathy could barely hear him.

"Owe me? What for?" She looked surprised.

"You saved my life, you got Bessie out of that house safely. And most importantly you saved yourself. You have been in a dangerous position among dangerous people. I understand why you ran away from them." His voice caught. He ran his hand through his hair.

"What I can't figure is why you ran away from me."

Cathy stood.

Her heartbeat slowed. Her eyes burned with unshed tears. She had learned from her family it was easier to run away from conflict than forebear belittlement or a slap in the face. But for the first time in her life she did not want to run away. This man. This beautiful, masculine, sexual man wanted her. She looked at the confusion in his luscious brown eyes, the muscular arms that had given her solace when she needed it. Then she realized. It was time to stop running and start building a life. And this was the man she wanted to build a life with. Her trembling stopped. Her eyes cleared to a soft blue-green. She looked directly into Ray's waiting eyes and said, "Because I love you."

Ray's face relaxed and he looked down. A deep chuckle rumbled in his chest. He rested his hands on his hips. He looked at this beautiful, brave, brilliant young woman.

'I must be crazy," he thought.

"I love you, too," he said and held out his arms for her.

A slow smile moved across Cathy's lips, but she stood her ground. There was one more thing she needed to clear up.

"In your letter you left for me before running away leaving me stuck in that white cottage in the middle of nowhere with no one to talk to except a woman who doesn't talk, you said you would decide what to do with me when you got back. What did you decide to do with me?"

For the first time since she opened her eyes in that brothel and saw Ray lying there naked beside her, he looked stumped.

Cathy continued.

"You need to know that you don't have to do anything with me. I am not one of your cows to be dealt with. I am a person. I make my own decisions. I am open to hearing what you have to say, then any dealings between us will be mutually decided upon. We will abide by mutual decisions. I just wanted you to know that up front, before you made your decision.

Ray blinked his eyes and stared at her for a moment.

"Yep. I am definitely crazy," he thought.

He cleared his throat.

"I don't remember saying that." He shuffled his feet. "But I do remember that shortly after you introduced yourself to me that night on the trail that you were running wild and some good man needed to get you under control."

"And you thought that man should be you?" Cathy asked.

"I thought I could use a good wife to help me with the ranch. I'm starting a new breeding program and a brave, strong partner would go a long way to help reach a successful outcome."

Cathy drew her brows together.

"Breeding? Do you like babies? Baby humans, I mean."

Ray's eyes widened.

"Are you trying to tell me something?"

Cathy thought a minute and answered, "not yet."

Ray's smile spread into an excited grin.

"That's it!" he declared. "We have our first mutual decision. We're getting married tonight. I'll arrange for the captain to perform the ceremony. We'll have a big party when we get back home at the ranch." Cathy laughed.

"That's just what I was thinking, too, but I don't have anything to wear but this old red dress."

Ray took her in his arms and said, "We'll think of something."

Cathy looked up at him in amusement.

"Together of course," he teased. In one quick flick of the wrist, Ray pulled the tab of sheet between Cathy's breasts. The sheet slid off her body pooling at her feet. Ray stood back to admire the beautiful woman standing before him.

"Do you want a son or a daughter?" he asked watching closely for her reply.

"One of each," she answered.

"That's a good start," he happily agreed.

Cathy ran to him and jumped into his strong, warm arms.

"God, I love you," Ray said.

"I love you, too," Cathy purred and pressed her lips to his.

Ray lifted Cathy and placed her gently on the bed where they reveled in the mutually enjoyed passion that they would treasure for the rest of their mutually happy lives.

The End

ABOUT THE AUTHOR

Phyllis Kerr, a native Texan, was born in San Antonio and moved with her family to Houston when she was one year old. Phyllis' mother loved to read historical romance novels especially in her favorite Regency genre. As soon as she could read, Phyllis fell in love with romance novels, too. Over the years, she has watched so many wonderful writers develop the genre into one of the most popular today. Phyllis wrote her novel as an homage and thank you to those past, present and future writers who carry on the tradition of Romance.

Phyllis grew up in Houston, attended Bellaire High School and made her home in the Clear Lake City area. She earned her Bachelor of Arts degree in Literature from The University of Houston—Clear Lake while helping her husband build a business and raising two sons. She has worked in the family business, taught English and English as a second language and now enjoys writing, spending time with her husband, two sons, three grandchildren and loving cat, ChaCho.

Made in the USA
Middletown, DE
24 December 2020

30109524R00128